THE MAGICAL PEPPERS

AND THE GREAT VANISHING ACT

First published in Great Britain by
HarperCollins *Children's Books* in 2012
HarperCollins *Children's Books* is a division of
HarperCollins*Publishers* Ltd,
77-85 Fulham Palace Road, Hammersmith, London W6 8JB

Visit us on the web at
www.harpercollins.co.uk

1

ISBN-978-0-00-743003-1

Printed and bound in England by
Clays Ltd, St Ives plc

THE MAGICAL PEPPERS

AND THE GREAT VANISHING ACT

SIÂN PATTENDEN

Illustrated by Jess Mikhail

HarperCollins *Children's Books*

The Troupe

Monty

Esmé

Uncle Potty

Henry J Henry

Queen

Contents

Dr Pompkins – Totality Magic

Welcome once more to *Dr Pompkins – Totality Magic* (expanded deluxe limited edition with velour cover and gold lettering).

Here you will find the best tricks and the most up-to-date advice. Since I last saw you, I have been trotting round the globe, performing at least four tricks a night to an eager audience. But it has taken its toll on my body. My legs are creaking, the old joints are barking and I also believe that I may be slightly deaf. Reader, I am getting old, so I want you to go forth, take the Pompkins baton, and perform the tricks included inside this book – at home, to friends and relatives, at school – and let's see that the bubble of magic never bursts.

In all totality,

Dr Pompkins

CHAPTER ONE

Magic Shed

*K*errr-flapp!

Esmé Pepper saw the letter arrive first, landing loudly on the doormat of the house at Highwood Road. It was addressed to Uncle Potty, but there was no clue as to the sender. The postmark was smudged and the address was printed, not handwritten. Esmé scratched her right ear and began to worry. She hoped it was not the letter that

had been threatened by the local council.

Kerrr-phoooow!

The sound of a small explosion coming from the garden made Esmé start. Her twin brother, Monty, and her uncle Potty, a professional magician, were outside, busy creating new magic tricks. Esmé put the letter in her trouser pocket and ran out to the recently fitted magic shed that Potty had been using over the last few weeks. Potty was standing alone, covered in soot. Only minutes ago, the shed had sported its clean, watertight roof. Now there were pieces of charred wood all over the grass and the entire roof was gone.

"Problem?" asked Esmé.

"Nothing that can't be fixed," answered Potty brightly.

"Where's Monty?"

"Here," came a voice, and Esmé looked up to see her brother, happily dangling upside down from a tree by his ankles. "I don't think we got it quite right, Uncle Potty."

"I'll go and get the ladder," said Esmé, rushing to the hall cupboard.

Twenty minutes later, a puzzled Montague Pepper was sitting on the grass, trying to work out what had gone wrong.

"We've spent two long weeks trying to make the shed disappear in the style of

Nigel Copperfield," he worried. "And all we've done is blow up the roof."

"It *will* happen," said Potty. "We just need to consult *Dr Pompkins – Totality Magic* again."

"Do you think Mr Copperfield reads Dr Pompkins?" asked Monty.

"Oh yes," said Potty, sitting down to join him. "We all do. It's our bible."

Esmé sat down with them. "Do you really think you can make the shed disappear?" she asked. "What props did you use for the trick?"

"A fire extinguisher, a piece of curtain, twenty-four packs of playing cards and a can of lemonade," replied Potty. "I think

the lemonade might have been the issue, don't you?"

"Surely," said Esmé, "the *issue* was with the fire extinguisher. Has it been safety checked? I think Mum and Dad have had it for ages."

Both Monty and Potty looked at each other. "Oh, so *that's* what it was," Potty said, turning to Esmé. "You know, I really hadn't thought about that until you mentioned it, Esmé, dear. Or maybe there were too many packs of cards."

Sensible Esmé gave Potty a knowing look. *Surely* he knew playing cards had never made anything explode in the whole history of the world. Ever.

Esmé wondered if the neighbours might complain about the exploding shed, which reminded her of the letter that was still in her pocket.

"You've had something through the post," she said, handing the envelope to Potty, whose normally pinkish face turned white in an instant.

"*Could it be…*" he asked out loud, his one eyebrow furrowed deep.

Monty trembled. Esmé frowned.

"*… from the council?*" asked Potty, trying to open the letter without his hands shaking too much. "I don't know what I will do if my wonderful shed is shut down. I will have nowhere to create my tricks in peace."

*

Uncle Potty had first hit upon the idea of a magic shed four weeks earlier. It would be a place of his own where he could try out and experiment with his tricks. So when Mr and Mrs Pepper had said he could build it in their garden, he was ecstatic. Monty would be on standby to help him at any time. It was perfect.

Once it was decided, Potty and the Pepper twins got a bus to the nearest garden centre and spent almost two hours deliberating on the best shed for the job. Some had heating, one came fitted with a plunge pool and another doubled as a noodle stall for rock festivals. In the end, Potty had plumped for a traditional shed with a sturdy front door and had it delivered the next day.

Esmé and Monty were both thrilled. Surely this was the solution to the problems associated with Potty practising in the house – no more baked beans on the living-room carpet, no more flooded bathrooms or tripping over wands on the stairs.

And yet... Esmé noticed that even in his own shed, Potty could not help but make either a lot of noise or a lot of mess. He managed to break the door off its hinges on the first day with an energetic silk scarf trick. On the second day, he annoyed the neighbours with a badly played trumpet solo, which he claimed was for an act involving *the magic of music.* Two local cats joined him and howled in unison, causing the woman down the road to ring the police to complain about the "Lady Gaga Tribute Act". When Potty tried to make the shed magically transform into an elephant, the noise was such that Esmé had to put her foot down. No more elephants.

Matters had come to a head a week ago when a small man from the local council called Jeremy, dressed in a tan corduroy suit, with sweatbands round his wrists, appeared at the house and proceeded to read Uncle Potty an official warning.

"If you continue to cause disruption to your neighbours, you will be fined and most

probably taken to court," he said sternly. "We at the council take these things very seriously because you are causing severe cress to others," he finished, and looked up from his clipboard.

"Cress?" asked Potty.

"*Cress to others*," replied Jeremy, wiping his forehead with his left-hand sweatband.

"Do you mean stress?" asked Monty, peering round Potty's elbow.

"Ahem, yes, *stress* to others," finished Jeremy, now wiping his forehead with his right-hand sweatband. "This is your final warming. That is, you have been warmed."

"*Warmed?*" asked Esmé, trying not to burst into laughter as Jeremy walked away.

Although they had chuckled about Jeremy and his *warming* after his departure, Esmé, Monty and Potty were deeply concerned. Potty was a creative type – he needed to be free in order to invent new, innovative tricks. If he was forced to keep the noise down, he might not be able to do his job; if he was taken to court, they might ban the magic shed altogether.

Fiddling with the seal, Potty took another few seconds breaking open the envelope. He breathed in slowly.

"It's an invitation," he said at last, with some relief. "'Mr Henry J. Henry invites the Potty Magician to perform for Her Majesty

the Queen at the Grand Royal Opening of Mr Henry's MEGA-MILLION SUPER MUSEUM in one week's time. RSVP in person by August the first at the latest.' That's the day after tomorrow," Potty added.

"Wow," said Monty.

"Is it real?" asked Esmé, taking the invitation and examining it.

"There's a gold stamp on it," said Monty, peering over her shoulder. "Of course it's real."

Potty was thrilled – he had made a name for himself after the triumphant show at the Sea Spray Theatre and had received regular bookings ever since. He had even

23

appeared on television a handful of times, including a small slot on *Abraca-Deborah* – a magic show featuring Pat Daniels and his fragrant wife – performing a trick with a dessert spoon and a toothpick. But on reading *this* invitation, Potty was happier than he had ever been – he had never dreamed of being asked to entertain on such an important occasion. Every frond of hair leaped up from the top of his head as if his fingers had been stuck in the mains. "I will perform for Her *actual* Majesty, a *royal* personage, in *real* life! It's a true honour."

"In all totality," added Monty, nodding.

Potty paused for a moment. "*Henry J.*

Henry – I'm sure I remember that name from somewhere…" He scratched his head and some hair fell on to the floor.

"I think he was once a member of the International Magic Guys Club. I'm certain that he went by the name of Harry Starfeathers – although he was so clumsy with his props that we used to call him Harry Butterfingers. Well well, if he isn't a high-flying museum curator these days, working closely with royalty."

All problems with the council were, at this point, forgotten. All thought of the accident with the shed roof was put aside too. The Potty Magician was to perform in front of the Queen in a week! Monty

started rehearsing what he called his *Junior Royal Bow.*

"Come along," said Potty. "We must decide what trick to perform at the Grand Royal Opening."

"What about one-handed tortoise juggling?" asked Monty. "I saw that on an American TV programme once."

"No no – too messy," replied Potty.

"I liked the trick you did where a playing card turns into flower petals," said Esmé.

"Zamiel's Rose?" answered Potty. "No, the Queen will have seen that one before – it's been done many times." He shifted on the grass. "This is not an easy task."

"Uncle P, what have we just been doing?"

"Worrying about the high-explosive properties of lemonade," said Potty, gazing up at the sky.

"Before that," prompted Monty.

"Trying to make the shed disappear."

"Exactly!" said Monty. "Why don't you make something from the museum disappear?"

"Great idea! Maybe a statue or something like that," suggested Esmé.

Potty stopped to think.

"Or should we be more ambitious?" mused the Potty Magician. "Anyone can make a statue disappear."

"We could bring the shed?" suggested Monty.

Potty was having a brainwave. "The Queen has seen the greatest performers the world has ever known. She will expect something incredible, out of the realms of possibility – a simple shed might not do the trick. Her Royal Highness saw Timothy Cooper rip a tablecloth from a dining table, under the nose of a giant bear that was just sitting down to enjoy a substantial meal. The plates and cutlery remained exactly where they had been set; the bear was happy and the crowd went wild. Anyway, *we* need a true spectacle that breaks new ground on a global scale – but without any bears, for safety reasons."

Monty thought for a moment. "Could

28

we make the Queen disappear?"

"I think that may be against the law," responded Esmé.

"One moment, Esmé and Monty," said Potty. "Maybe we could make the *museum* disappear. What do you think? It's going to be a tough one to pull off, but if Nigel Copperfield can make the Egyptian pyramids vanish for a few seconds, then I can certainly dispose of this so-called *Mega-Million Super Museum*."

"Even though the museum is vast and heavy and real?" asked Esmé.

"Oh yes."

Esmé truly hoped that Potty *could* make the museum disappear. He hadn't done

very well with the shed, but they had just over a week to rehearse the grand trick, so there was a chance it might actually work.

Potty looked closely at the invitation that he was still clutching in his hand.

"We need to RSVP in person the day after tomorrow. That gives us one whole day to sort out the nuts and bolts of our act."

"It also means I can spend tomorrow at the library researching," said Esmé happily. "The museum has been standing for decades. It's only in the past few weeks that it's been reinvented as the Mega-Million Super Museum. I might be able to find some details about the building and the floor plan so that you can work out your trick in advance, Potty."

"Sounds splendid! We are set – nothing can go wrong with a little preparation! We *will* make the museum disappear."

An excerpt from

Dr Pompkins – Totality Magic

TRICK: Möbius Magic

You will need paper, Sellotape and scissors for this trick. Tell your audience you have made a loop out of paper to put round your wrist, but it won't fit. "Stone me," you'll say, "I'll just cut the loop bigger!" Your clever audience will laugh as they know you cannot make a loop bigger just by cutting it.

———

However, if you cut the loop in half up the middle, instead of into two loops, you will now have one larger loop.

The secret is that your original loop is actually a *Möbius Strip* – a mathematical marvel – made from a strip of paper that has been twisted once and then taped together {see fig. 1}.

Health and Safety

Health and Safety is not something to be frowned upon. Please do not try to work with fire, big cats or swords. You are still a beginner and you can never be too careful – some ambitious tricks can cause an accident unless handled by an experienced professional. Construct your own props with Sellotape and scissors rather than hammer and nails. Cotton wool, also, is rather soft and forgiving. The great Pat Daniels always liked to construct his own props, but one day he managed to slice off his own pinky finger with a circular saw. Ouch!

In all totality,

Dr Pompkins

CHAPTER TWO

Henry J. Henry

"It's gigantic. How on *earth* are we going to make it disappear?"

Monty Pepper was taken aback at how vast the museum seemed as he, Esmé and Potty walked through the tall, iron entrance gates. Monty wore a new red cape over his velvet magician's suit; Potty was in a yellow satin number worn over a tweed suit. Esmé wore her light summer cagoule (ready for

35

all weathers), which had a large pocket. In it she carried a penknife, a small torch and a packet of strawberry chews, just in case anyone got hungry. Everyone was prepared to meet Henry J. Henry and see inside this inspiring Mega-Million Super Museum.

The building was impressive – enormous stone pillars supported the Greek-style triangular roof. The museum was at least the size of a football pitch plus a department store on the side. It stood, a triumph of traditional, imposing, stone-clad building-ness.

"It must be very old," Monty said.

"Construction work was finished in

eighteen fifty-three and took over two decades," said Esmé. "I read about it at the library."

The Peppers and Potty walked alongside the flourishing garden at the front – even the outside was part of the new museum. Here were *Plants from Really Really Ancient Times* – a display that included *Welwitschia* from the Namibia desert, a shrub that can live for up to two thousand years.

Potty raised his eyebrow. "Better not make that disappear," he said.

They walked to the entrance, up a flight of grand stone steps that were being scrubbed furiously by around

twenty cleaners in white coats.

"That's a lot of cleaning," remarked Monty.

At once, a beam of bright white light hit the central column, followed by a pulsating strobe of purple to the right-hand side of the building. The visitors stopped in their tracks. Loud music pumped from large speakers at each side of the museum, with deep bass notes and some toppy hi-hats.

"Technical rehearsal, light show number one," shouted a man, who wore a safety helmet and had an orange vest over his clothes. "Cue the lasers."

Esmé, Monty and Potty gasped as the words MEGA-MILLION ROYAL OPENING appeared in mid-air before them. The laser display then changed to the words HER ROYAL HIGHNESS, then formed into an image of a crown, which slowly morphed into the outline of a corgi.

"OK, that's enough for now," said the man in the hard hat, and the lasers stopped at once.

"Impressive," said Monty. "Do you think they'll put *your* name in lasers for the opening, Potty?"

Uncle Potty furrowed his brow, not used to the notion of celebrity. "Maybe."

"As the light show suggests," said Esmé seriously, "this is *more* than a normal museum; this truly *is* a *Mega-Million Super* museum."

The grand opening was clearly a big operation. By the main entrance was a poster of the Queen wearing her ceremonial robes and a huge crown. She was not smiling in the picture. Star Attraction! read the poster.

THE MUSEUM'S GRAND OPENING WILL SHOWCASE...
HER MAJESTY THE QUEEN'S REGAL JEWEL COLLECTION.

CAST YOUR EYES UPON A SELECTION OF
THE MOST EXQUISITE JEWELS
AND HIGHLY PRIZED TRINKETS
FROM HER MAJESTY THE QUEEN'S
OWN PERSONAL TREASURE TROVE.

"Ooh," said Monty.

The Peppers and Potty stepped inside. There was a slow *smoosh!*, and a puff of dry ice enveloped them all as if they were on a film set.

"I want to live here," cooed Monty. "It's amazing."

Someone passed by, pushing a small trolley filled with USB sticks and mouse mats. Each had a picture of a transparent skull on it.

"What are they for?" asked Monty.

"For sale, maybe," said Esmé. "Does the museum have a shop?"

"Of course it does, old sport," came a voice from the midst of the dry ice. A hand

appeared through the fug of smoke, then an arm, then a man.

"Henry J. Henry," the man introduced himself to Uncle Potty. He was tall and wore a light grey suit. "Pleased to make your acquaintance. I guess you are the Potty Magician."

Henry smiled at them all – he seemed almost like an angel, thought Esmé, appearing from a celestial cloud.

Henry looked at Esmé and Monty. "And you must be...?"

"My niece and nephew," said Potty, "Esmé and Monty Pepper."

Monty sniffed the air. "What's that nice smell?"

"Must be my aftershave, *Toujours, Matey.*"

Henry gazed down at the children. "I do hope you like our little museum here. We have made use of technology to create a sensational experience. And we want the experience to be experiential, if you see what I mean." Henry smiled again and his teeth sent out a gleam that Esmé thought could have blinded a small animal such as a shrew or a weasel. The clothes Henry wore were expensive and his hair was smoothed back and sleek. He was one of those people who looked as if he was successful at everything – that all he touched turned to gold. Esmé imagined that Henry J. Henry lived in a mansion that was filled every day with fresh-cut flowers, that he drank champagne from small golden flutes and bathed in goat's milk when he fancied it.

The dry ice dispersed.

"Welcome to our world, Potty Magician and young relatives," said Henry. "The Mega-Million Super Museum is at your disposal."

Then Potty spoke. "We've met before, Mr Henry. Weren't you once a member of the International Magic Guys Club?"

"My, yes, I was," said Henry, looking back intently at Potty. "But I don't seem to recall..."

"Not to worry, I was just a whipper-snapper," Potty said. "Wasn't Harry Starfeathers your stage name?"

Henry J. Henry looked a little put out that Potty had such a good memory.

"Um, yes. But I got out of the magic business a while ago. There was too much pressure," he muttered.

"Well, that's a shame," said Potty, deciding not to mention Henry's nickname – *Butterfingers*.

"I never really had the talent," continued Henry, "to charm with magic, to entertain. It's a gift, I tell you, old sport. A gift."

"There's always something to improve on, or something new to try," explained Potty humbly. "You can't be left behind. Each trick must be better than the last."

Henry sighed deeply. "It's so nice to catch

up. Anyway, we must talk turkey."

Potty nodded. "The trick?"

"Yes, the trick," replied Henry. "The Queen has personally invited you to perform at the Mega-Million Super Museum opening. Apparently she saw you on television and loved your act. She contacted me especially to put you on the bill for next week's grand event."

Esmé could see that Henry was stressing the fact that it was the Queen's idea to invite Potty to perform.

"I am certainly a lucky magician," said Potty.

"So, what sort of thing have you got in mind for the show?" Henry asked.

"Well, as you know a little bit about magic, I think you'll understand when I say that I want to create an epic performance," replied Potty. "Something truly memorable. So... I'd like to make the museum disappear, if that's all right with you."

"I see," said Henry thoughtfully. "Yes, yes, that should be fine."

Esmé and Monty glanced at each other. They had expected Mr Henry to react with a little more enthusiasm – or at least surprise. Uncle Potty was suggesting that he make the building vanish – not make a rabbit leap out from a top hat.

"The trick is based on those performed by Nigel Copperfield," explained Potty,

47

thinking that Henry's slow reaction was just one of caution. "Nigel made the Statue of Liberty vanish once, if you recall. I'd like to use his methods."

Henry was silent for a little longer, but soon he started beaming. "Mr Potty, I think it's a superb idea. It certainly would attract a lot of attention… but you will be able to bring the museum back, won't you, old sport?"

"Of course," said a delighted Potty.

"Let me think," said Henry. "You'll have to perform the trick outside – create a bit of atmosphere, wave a wand around, then – *whoosh!* – the museum vanishes, at least to the naked eye."

Potty nodded.

Henry paused again. Esmé could see that he was thinking through each detail in his mind.

"What I suggest," said Henry at last, "is that making the museum disappear is all well and good, but we could add a little something extra."

Potty looked intrigued.

"How about," continued Henry, "a *taster* version of the trick, to whet the audience's appetite for the main event? I suggest you make a small object disappear first – pretending that this is the sole performance – until you suddenly and unexpectedly make the museum disappear. Catching the audience off guard like that will give the whole trick the *wow* factor."

Potty raised his one furry eyebrow. "*Wow* factor. I hadn't thought of that," he said. "It's a wonderful idea."

"We would just have to choose the first object," said Henry, as someone with another trolley holding skull-shaped pencil sharpeners passed by.

Here, Esmé piped up. "We could use something from the museum – something ancient and special and magical... if that's all right, Mr Henry."

Monty agreed. "Good plan – it would give it a theme."

"Yes," answered Henry. "Ancient, special

and magical; that would be excellent."

"A pencil sharpener?" Monty suggested.

"Would that be magical?" asked Esmé. "Or even ancient?"

"I was thinking we could find a really old one."

"I've an idea," said Esmé, remembering the laser display outside the museum. "How about the crown?"

"Or maybe a mummified head?"

"Didn't I just see a crystal skull on a mouse mat?" asked Potty.

"You can't make a mouse mat disappear; that wouldn't be very exciting," said Monty.

"No no!" said Potty. "A piece of *crystal*

would be marvellous – it would cast a magical light – but it must not be too large and awkward to disappear."

"Incredible," said Henry, his eyes wide. "You have all come up with the answer yourselves."

Esmé wondered what Henry J. Henry meant by this. Of *course* they had come up with the answer – they were planning Potty's show.

"I have something that is exactly what you need – an item that is part of the Royal Collection. A crystal skull. It *is* ancient, magical and special. Not only that, it is worth millions."

"Well, we can try something else if it's too

precious," said Potty. "I wouldn't want to—"

"No no no, I insist you use it," said Henry, a broad smile on his lips.

"We would take good care of it," promised Monty.

"It sounds perfect," said Potty, holding out his hand. "Let's shake on it, Mr Henry. This is going to blow the Queen's socks off."

Henry seemed delighted. "I've always thought that with other rivals – I mean, other *magicians* – the best thing is to pool ideas."

Esmé noticed Henry J. Henry suddenly blush and trail off. Did he just say *rivals*? Surely he didn't see Potty as competition any more? Mr Henry was a successful museum curator, not an entertainer.

"Can we see this crystal skull?" asked Monty.

"Yes, I will have to check it for size and weight," said Potty.

"We can go and look at it now, if you like," said Henry, regaining his composure. "I can show you the Wealth and Wisdom Zone, which houses the Royal Collection."

"Marvellous," said Potty, guiding the children with his long arms as Henry led the way. The throbbing mass of cleaners, who were busy sweeping and polishing the floor, simultaneously parted as Henry walked through the main hall.

"He seems most enthusiastic. A fine fellow," Uncle Potty murmured to the twins.

Monty nodded.

"Glance upwards, young sports!" Henry called to the Peppers, walking behind him. In so doing, Esmé and Monty both saw a number people in white lab coats dangling from the ceiling. They were also armed with broomsticks and were trying to polish the ceiling. No expense, it seemed, had been spared for this royal opening.

An excerpt from

Dr Pompkins – Totality Magic

TRICK: Magic Bottle

Kindly and in your best loud voice, ask for a volunteer from the audience. Show him or her an empty bottle, then *drop drop drop* your magic wand inside, noting how easily it falls in.

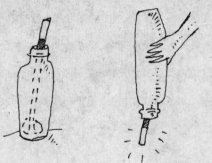

Your volunteer will gasp "Crikey!" as you turn the bottle upside down and the wand magically remains suspended inside.

The clue is in a *dark-coloured* bottle and a pencil eraser that you have in your pocket. After you have shown your volunteer the empty bottle, slip the eraser inside it without anyone seeing – you must practise your sleight of hand skills here. Drop the wand into the bottle and push it into the eraser.

Now turn it upside down VERY SLOWLY and mumble all sorts of enchantments while you're doing this. Pull on the wand slightly when the bottle is turning over so the piece of eraser gets wedged into the opening. You'll need to practise this a few times, my magical friends.

———

HEY PRESTO! The wand doesn't fall out. It's magic and full-time entertainment, wand-style.

The Library

Once, there were libraries on every street corner with young readers (and older too) hopping about, arms filled with books, thrilled to be taking them home to read and enjoy. Now you'd be hard-pressed to find a library in many towns, let alone a nice independent bookseller. Someone perched upon a high ledge on the mountainside of Government decided that no one needed books, but I, Dr Pompkins, Magical Conjuror and Spiritual Adviser In All Totality, must stand up for libraries. If you happen to be near one of the few that they haven't managed to close down yet, then please use it and borrow some magic books. Glancing at other people's ideas is good for your brain and will expand your repertoire. Not everyone can afford to buy the latest magic guide, and a library gives you access within reasonable opening hours.

In all totality,

Dr Pompkins

CHAPTER THREE

Big Ruffled Collars

Henry led the Pepper twins and Potty into a brightly lit room that had low flute music playing in the background. On the right-hand wall was a row of buttons that made GENUINE SOUNDS FROM THE ELIZABETHAN ERA. Monty was delighted at the very thought of things to press, and lingered behind.

Esmé listened as one marked BASE METAL TURNING TO GOLD produced a sound quite

61

similar to that of a cement mixer. Another noise – DEFEATING THE SPANISH ARMADA – was a bit like carrots being grated. Monty's favourite was BIG RUFFLED COLLARS, which he pressed repeatedly. It sounded like a cat scratching a doorframe.

"It's interactive," Monty said to his sister.

"I know," said Esmé. "It still doesn't explain why a ruffled collar sounds like a cat's claws, though."

"I think it's brilliant in here. When it opens, I'm going to visit every day."

"But you go to school from Monday to Friday."

"*After* school. And at weekends."

"I thought you were going to practise in

the magic shed at weekends."

"Er, let's go and join the others," said Monty quickly. "We need to keep up with Henry J. Henry."

"Come along," the museum boss called to the children. "We haven't got all day."

Esmé had just noticed one of the items she had seen in the library book – a round object of shiny black stone – displayed in a glass cabinet. Esmé wondered why they couldn't stay and look at the exhibits for a little while longer.

"Is this the obsidian mirror?" she asked Henry, pointing to the object.

Henry turned reluctantly and walked back towards her.

"Yes, but we haven't much—"

"I've read all about it," Esmé explained with great enthusiasm. "It's said to have real magical qualities – it can predict the future. Dr John Dee had it brought back from South America – he was Queen Elizabeth the First's mystical adviser, wasn't he."

Henry looked at Esmé. "Well, that's great that you know so much about it, young sport."

"I found Dr Dee very interesting," said Esmé, "because he tried to make a science out of magic and spiritualism. He communicated with spirits and it's said that his guardian angel predicted the

Gunpowder Plot of sixteen o five. The mirror itself became famous."

"Well, the crystal skull has a lot of history behind it too," snapped Henry. "That's the object your uncle Potty is going to use, isn't it? Not a mirror."

"But it's interesting to look at the other exhibits on our way to the skull," said Esmé, disappointed that they were being moved on.

Henry, realising he had snapped, smiled at Esmé. "You will love the skull, you really will. It has so much history."

But now Esmé wasn't sure how sincere Henry was being. Wasn't he interested in the other items in the Mega-Million

Super Museum? This was a bit surprising, considering he was in charge of the whole place.

"Isn't there some sort of code attached to the mirror?" she asked Henry.

"*Code?*"

"I read that Sir Hans Toast, who founded the original museum over a hundred years ago, devised symbols that were used as a map to access some parts of the museum – secret passageways, I think it said."

Hearing this, Monty looked closely at the exhibit. "There's some funny writing on the information panel – is that it?"

Henry looked at the Pepper twins with a steely expression. "You certainly are two very bright young things, aren't you. However, the idea of a code is rubbish. Those symbols are for the... um... audio tour."

"But..." said Esmé, then trailed off.

"Now, onward, everybody," said Henry, putting a manicured hand behind Esme's back and simply pushing her forward. "Let's get to this exciting crystal skull. We haven't got all day."

Esmé, Potty and Monty followed the museum boss. "Marvellous, isn't it," enthused Potty. "The museum – all these objects from the past making history come alive. It inspires me, Esmé, it truly does."

"I wish we hadn't been moved along so

quickly. I would have liked to stay and make a sketch of the mirror."

"If Henry wants us to hurry, there must be a reason," said Potty, always respectful of people who were the boss of places, like museums.

They passed a room full of Egyptian mummies.

"These seem interesting," remarked Monty, but Henry did not hear him and continued walking. Esmé, however, had spotted another object she'd read about and she was not going to pass this one by without having a good look.

"It's the Rosetta Bone. It's famous throughout the world."

Potty called out to Henry to stop for a moment, and he did, albeit with a rather fake grin.

"It's an *incredible* piece of Egyptian history," said Esmé excitedly. "It has all these hieroglyphs – symbols that represent letters of the alphabet – carved into it."

Monty walked up and peered at the bone, which was standing alone, without a display cabinet to protect it. "Is it a dinosaur bone?"

Potty stroked his chin. "Of course it's not." Then he turned to Esmé. "Is it?"

Esmé had read all about it during her fact-finding mission in the library.

"It's the hind leg of an ancient cow.

Decoding the bone has been vital to the understanding of Egyptian life and world history too."

Henry yawned. Was he making fun of Esmé? Had she been too swotty? Esmé was silently annoyed – she wanted to say something, but felt she couldn't.

Potty instinctively went to tap the bone, then stopped himself, knowing that you weren't meant to touch objects in museums, that they were fragile and sensitive and could crumble under a whisper.

"Oh, go on," said Henry, seeing Potty pause. "Handle it all you want. Pick it up, move it around. It's just an old bone."

And Henry J. Henry walked off without waiting for the others.

Monty glanced at Esmé. "Well, he is the boss."

Esmé looked down at her shoes, a little dejected. "I just thought it was really interesting."

Dr Pompkins – Totality Magic

TRICK: Into Thin Air

For this trick you will need an ordinary deck of cards, a handkerchief with a hem, a toothpick and scissors.

Take the toothpick and cut it so that it's the same size as the width of a playing card. Poke it into the hem of the handkerchief, making sure it won't fall out. Now you can perform.

Take a deck of cards and spread them out on a table, then bring out the handkerchief and say, "I will make an ordinary playing card disappear, right before your very eyes, oh yes – because I am a magician in all totality." Or something similar.

Place the handkerchief on top of the pile of cards, with the toothpick section underneath the rest of the handkerchief. Look casual as you do this, as if you were thinking about your dinner. Maybe chat about the weather or the plumage of the mandarin duck. Next, using one hand, lift the toothpick between your thumb and forefinger and raise it up from the pile of cards – it should appear as if you are holding the edge of one of the cards.

Then with a flick of the wrist and an "In all totality!" you wave the handkerchief in the air to show there's no card inside. It has simply vanished.

Huzzah!

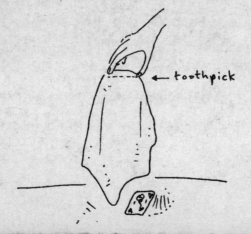

← toothpick

Voice and Tone, Volume and Accents

People say that your accent reveals a lot about you. It might display where you are from, what type of school you go to and what sort of opera you like. Well, tish now, if you are a performer, you can alter your voice to suit your *persona* (for more on *personas*, see *Dr Pompkins* Volumes I and II, non-deluxe versions). I know one magician who adopts a rough Scottish accent when he is on stage as he feels it gives him a more *earthy* image. He does, of course, go by the name of the Scottish Magician. Another conjuror often pretends to be French when she does her tablecloth routine – to marvellous effect. There are many ways to project the voice – as some great actors will tell you – so that people at the back can hear. You might want to seek out an actor's guide in a local shop, or indeed library, and read it through for ideas.

In all totality,

Dr Pompkins

CHAPTER FOUR

The Crystal Skull

Esmé, Monty and Potty walked along yet another corridor, the walls of which were lit from below with tiny ice-blue lights and filled once more with white-coated cleaners scrubbing at the marble floor.

Esmé looked around, thinking back to the stories about Sir Hans Toast's code and the secret passageways. Toast had created the museum all those years ago with his

own vast collection of objects from around the world, so the library book had said. He had designed the museum so there were underground passageways and rooms to store some of the items that were not on show. Toast's special code had been discovered a decade ago, written on the information panels belonging to a handful of objects scattered around the museum. The code was still hidden, but it would tell anyone *in the know* where the secret passageways were.

But Henry claimed he was not aware of the code. Was he telling the truth?

Certainly on this level there was no sign of an underground passageway – no doors leading off anywhere, no secret levers or pulleys. (Esme's speciality was using levers and pulleys if Potty needed technical help with his stage act.) Just clean white walls and hi-tech lighting.

At last Henry led them into a large room with a neon sign on the wall that read, in bright-red tubes of light: WEALTH AND WISDOM ZONE.

"Now *this* is what we're most proud of, this is what the modern public wants." Henry held his arms out wide. "A spectacular display of the nation's most treasured articles."

"The Royal Collection?" Esmé remembered the poster.

"Yes, Her Majesty has lent us most of the treasures, which is really very good of her. Potty, you'll get so much inspiration from here."

The Wealth and Wisdom Zone was the largest single exhibition space inside the museum – it was clearly designed to attract the most visitors.

"Everyone loves the Queen, don't they?" said Henry. "And people like gazing at large slabs of jewellery and exotic gems, especially with the addition of modern lighting and laser displays."

With this, Henry J. Henry dimmed the lights.

"This is what I wanted to show you," he

called in the darkness. "Forget about the other mouldy old exhibits, you're in for a treat here."

At once, a spotlight shone to the left, directly on what looked like a wall of pure gold bullion. The spotlight swung quickly to the right, where it alighted on an enormous ruby, the size of an ostrich egg (and a particularly large ostrich at that).

Monty couldn't help letting out a large gasp; Potty squeaked in awe; Esmé was silent.

The light swung back into the centre of the room and illuminated an empty velvet-covered table.

Potty squeaked again, only to realise that

what he was looking at was just an empty space.

"Wait a moment," said Henry, and he clicked his fingers as a piece of heavy damask fabric fell on to the table from above. Henry counted to three and the fabric swiftly rose to reveal a table full of treasures – a royal crown holding gems as fat as digestive biscuits, next to a wildly twinkling sceptre. Scattered around were diamonds the size of chicken nuggets and something that looked like a gold cheese grater.

"Wow," said Monty, who had never imagined he would *imagine* seeing anything like it in his life, let alone actually *see* it.

"A golden cheese grater."

"It's wonderful," said Esmé, whose eyes were hurting just watching the jewels sparkling under the lights.

"And it's all worth a lot of money," said Henry.

Potty was silent, dumbstruck by the jewels.

"Now, wait for the next part," said Henry.

The light suddenly went out, then shone once more on the gold bullion, then the ruby, then the Crown Jewels. It repeated the cycle speedily, in quick succession. Again and again, the light switched from one great show of wealth to another. It was almost hypnotic. The light went out again

and a new object was illuminated at the far end of the room.

"Whoa," mumbled Potty.

"In all totality," added Monty.

The Peppers and Potty walked towards the great shining object in the distance. It cast small lines of coloured light in all directions.

"This is the *pièce de résistance* – the crystal skull," said Henry, now enthusiastic. "It's thought to have been made by Mayan stone workers in Mexico hundreds of years ago. It's carved from a single block of quartz."

The skull retained the light within its crystal form, making the object look as if it glowed from the inside.

"It certainly is impressive," noted Potty.

"And *unlike* the boring old obsidian mirror," said Henry, "this is the object that is said to contain *real* magic. Whoever owns the skull will be blessed with good fortune – *extreme wealth*, in fact."

"I just saw it wink," said Monty.

"Maybe it's the angle of the light," suggested Esmé.

Monty continued to gaze at the skull, wondering if it would bring him luck and extra pocket money to buy more magic tricks with.

"Of all the items in this room," said Henry J. Henry with pride, "the skull is worth the most money."

"I bet," said Monty.

"Yes," Henry's eyes lit up. "More, even, than the royal crown over there."

"But clearly that's not the point, is it?" Esmé looked hard at Henry, but he ignored her and turned to Potty.

"So you will use the skull in your trick, won't you?"

"Oh yes, most certainly," replied Potty, full of rapture. "It's the ideal object. It will capture the light beautifully and provide an aura of mystique that I would not have with an ordinary item, such as a hat or a pencil sharpener."

Esmé did not know what was *really* going on with Henry J. Henry, but something

about him was making her uneasy. She hadn't liked the way he'd yawned at the Rosetta Bone, amongst many *many* other things, and she was *determined* to be on high alert from now on.

An excerpt from

Dr Pompkins – Totality Magic

TRICK: The Disappearing Coin

This is a simple trick – all you need is a coin.

Sit at a table and tell your audience to hand you any coin they please. Tell them that you will be rubbing the coin on your elbow to make it disappear – then rub the coin on your left elbow.

Drop the coin on the table, and this time tell the assembled crowd that it doesn't seem to work with that elbow, so you will try with the other. Pick the coin up with your right hand and pretend to place it in your left hand. Put your right hand

(with the coin) up by your ear and rub your left hand – which your audience believe is holding the coin – on your elbow. Meanwhile, slowly drop the coin down the back of your shirt.

Display both of your hands and show the audience that you have made the coin disappear. *Voilissimo!* That will get 'em.

Tip: do not immediately stand up after this trick as the coin may fall on to the floor, revealing all.

Sewing and Handicraft

Many of you youngsters will be used to buying trousers and hats and T-shirts and trainers from shops ready-made. Yet, as a magician, you may have to go to Ye Olde Crafte Shoppe and get yourself a needle, thread and fabric – you will have to learn to sew and make. Many magicians hand-stitch their own costumes because they want something original to wear that simply *cannot* be bought off-the-peg. Many sew extra pockets into hats (see Eggs from a Hat trick) or trousers or waistcoats – to store or hide tiny magical props. Some magicians build their own props (see Health and Safety) and tricks. So thread up, prong through and get sewing!

In all totality,

Dr Pompkins

CHAPTER FIVE

Optical Illusion

At this point, the tour – such as it was – finished. Henry smiled. "I will leave you to your rehearsals," he said. "Do holler if you need anything." And he left the Wealth and Wisdom Zone, his shiny shoes squeaking on the marble floor beneath him. Uncle Potty and the Pepper twins decided to discuss Potty's trick outside on the grass, near the *Plants from Really Really*

Ancient Times. It was a bright sunny day, just the right sort of weather for talking through tricks.

Potty sat, deep in ponderous thought, although he was also able to produce a flask of tea from his yellow cape and three plastic cups at the same time.

"The skull is the right size and a good weight – I can make it disappear, no problem. What we need to do now is go back home and consult Dr Pompkins for tips," Potty mused. "Plus the Nigel Copperfield memoirs and some old International Magic Guys programmes. Then we come back tomorrow morning and start rehearsals. We have five days until the royal opening."

"Will the magic shed be involved?" asked Esmé, slightly concerned.

"It will be essential," answered Potty.

"What's my role?" asked Monty.

"Let me see..." replied Potty, standing up on the short grass. "We will need to make a plump cushion for the skull to rest on, so we'll visit the haberdasher's on the way back and buy some metres of fabric. Thenceforth –" Esmé could tell from Potty's language that he was truly inspired – "you, Montague Gaia Pepper, will be in charge of the cushion."

"Ooh," said Monty – whose middle name *was* indeed Gaia – and his eyes looked twice as big as normal.

94

"Esmé Moonchild Pepper," said Potty, unaware that Esmé might not be so keen on *her* full name being spoken out loud in public. "I want you to double-check the angles from the audience's point of view. And to ensure that nothing explodes this time."

"Rightio," said Esmé.

"This is a royal occasion, and therefore we must excel ourselves so that the Queen is proud of her regional performers," announced Potty.

"In all totality!" Monty cheered.

"To John Lewis we go!" shouted Potty and off the three marched, gleefully striding out of the tall museum gates and up the road.

Esmé quickly looked back at the colossal building as they left. She was certain she spotted Henry J. Henry looking out of a high window, watching the visitors depart.

Potty rehearsed in the magic shed day and night for four days. During his tea breaks he read his way through enormous volumes such as *75 Ways to Lose a Skyscraper, My Favourite Empty Spaces, Make Your Own Head Disappear* and many more.

To begin with, Potty tried to make a matchstick vanish and, due to his now exceptional sleight of hand skills – and his supremely long fingers – he succeeded.

Next, Potty made a large pot full of soil disappear. Easy. Then next door's cat. *Miaow.*

It took Potty a *whole* day to read Nigel Copperfield's memoirs, which were entitled *How to Marry a Supermodel*. Copperfield was famous for having asked a celebrated fashion model to be his wife while he was suspended from the Forth Bridge in Scotland. The bridge had disappeared during the proposal, leaving Nigel hanging in mid-air, which had impressed Miss Germaine Hoode so much she had said yes. The trouble was, Miss Hoode herself disappeared only moments after her loving reply, never to be found again.

The book didn't really contain tips for the professional magician, but was more of a long rambling lament from Nigel, who claimed that his life (and his magic skills) had never been the same since. Had Potty known that from the start, he would never have picked up the book in the first place.

"What a magnificent waste of time," Potty sighed, as he snapped the book shut. "At least I know not to mix magic with romance."

Esmé shuddered at the thought as Potty took a sheet of paper from the kitchen table and began to draw his plans for an elliptical frame.

"The frame must be big and almost

as tall as the museum," said Potty. "The audience will be seated outside, in front of the museum, watching my act through the frame; then a gigantic curtain will *swoosh!* across it for a couple of seconds. When the curtain is drawn back it will look like the museum has completely disappeared."

"How does that work?" asked Monty.

"It's complicated, so bear with me," explained Potty. "It's all in the lighting. We perform the trick at nightfall and use spotlights on the museum building and lights on the frame. We switch off all the lights when the curtain goes across and the museum is hidden. Then the next part of the act is that the frame itself will move and, according to Copperfield, the audience won't notice. When the curtain draws back it reveals the night sky – the museum is hidden by the enormous, brightly lit frame. It's all an optical illusion, but on a grand scale."

"So the *frame* does all the work," said Esmé.

"Exactly," replied Potty. "And because it's such a big frame and so brightly lit, it will obscure the museum completely. The angles have to be just so, but it should work."

"Wow," said Monty.

"Nigel Copperfield has made most of the world's famous landmarks disappear, so everybody who witnesses such a spectacle has the *expectation* that grand things will

happen. The result is that they willingly accept the illusion."

"Will you need this frame for the disappearance of the skull?" asked Esmé.

"No," replied Potty, "I just hide it in my cape when no one's looking."

Potty and Monty grabbed the piece of paper and took it into the garden so they could work on making the magic shed disappear.

"Give us thirty minutes and we'll show you something *incredible*, Esmé," said Monty.

"Actually, it could take up to an hour," corrected Potty.

Esmé sat patiently at the kitchen table and looked through the Nigel Copperfield memoir, though she was not really reading the book but thinking about Henry J. Henry. She wondered why he had no interest in the Rosetta Bone or Dr Dee's obsidian mirror. And hadn't he called Potty a *rival* instead of a *magician*? Hmm. Something just didn't add up.

After ten minutes, Monty ran into the kitchen to grab a pencil and Esmé realised that this was her chance to tell him about Henry. But once Esmé had explained her doubts, her twin brother seemed only vaguely concerned.

"Henry J. Henry only wanted to show us the skull," he explained. "*We* made him give us a tour – I think he was in a rush. He

has a whole show to put on in less than a week. Of course he didn't want to look at the other items on display."

"But I told you, he also called other magicians *rivals*, by mistake," Esmé said.

"A habit from his Harry Starfeather days?" ventured Monty. "Surely they *were* rivals when he was starting out, but I can't imagine Henry thinks that now."

Esmé was not convinced. There was something about Henry J. Henry she just didn't like.

"Come along, Esmé, we're ready for you!" called Potty from the garden. It was mid-evening already and the sun was starting to set.

"Don't worry," said Monty, patting Esmé on the shoulder. "Once you've seen Potty's act you'll forget about Henry."

Esmé smiled faintly and took her seat in the garden.

Dr Pompkins – Totality Magic

TRICK: Magic Cloak

There is a wonderful trick by the great Timothy Cooper that is simplicity itself, which he made famous by *failing* to conceal how it works. Cooper's genius lay in the fact that he realised the audience would laugh and enjoy themselves even if the tricks he was doing *didn't* succeed.

My friends, sew yourself a large cloak with sleeves and greet the audience wearing it. Make sure the fit is big.

Cooper's trick was to stand at the back of the stage by the curtain partition, and from his magic cloak he would produce items that got more and more

ridiculous: a bucket, a plank of wood, a ladder. Then his cloak would rip as he turned to talk to his assistant, who was behind the curtain, and the audience's enjoyment and laughter increased. They enjoyed the *failure of the illusion*.

If you have access to the internet you can watch Cooper's TV clips and learn from the master.

Noises from the Crowd

It is a pleasure and a wonder to enchant an audience and hear them sigh when the drama of each trick unfolds. Some of the audience will be rapt – some may be trying to find out what the weather is like in Poland on a smartphone or somesuch – but it's most important that at least they are all sitting in their seats. Babies might cry, children may fidget, but as long as you can involve them in the act – ask a few on stage to help you hold props or recite a magic catchphrase – all will be well. The clue to this is _experience_. Keep performing in front of your friends for practice. _Practice maketh perfection_, as they say.

In all totality,

Dr Pompkins

CHAPTER SIX

Plump Velvet Cushion

"**Y**ou did it!"

Esmé was astonished, even though she had been told earlier how the trick worked.

In the blink of an eye – or maybe even *half* a blink – Potty had actually made the magic shed disappear. Then after a few seconds the shed reappeared and Potty jumped four times on the spot with glee. If he could make the museum disappear in a similar way, he would perform a sensational trick that would go down in the history books.

"It works!" Potty shouted. "We *can* make this happen!"

Monty grinned as Esmé went to get a packet of biscuits from the kitchen to celebrate.

"We are ready," sighed Potty, contentedly sitting on the grass, after his fifth Hob Nob.

"Bring on the royal event," said Monty.

"In all totality," added Esmé.

Four days later, in the early evening, Potty and the Pepper twins arrived at the Mega-Million Super Museum for the dress rehearsal, but

found that the place was deserted. Unlike before, there were no cleaners to be seen, no lighting technicians or other workers trying not to fall from the ceiling. The Peppers and Uncle Potty walked up the smooth stone steps and into the building. Each was rather nervous: Potty's eyebrow kept twitching and Monty was chewing his fingernails.

"I had a nightmare last night," admitted Monty. "The Queen put me in the Tower of London because she didn't like Potty's trick. Then she cut off my head. It rolled about, then started performing mind-magic on a beefeater."

As they neared the top of the steps, Henry J. Henry appeared. Potty gently

pulled him to one side and Esmé watched as they spoke.

"I've practised the trick," said the Potty Magician. "And I'm extremely happy with it."

Henry smiled, his extra-shiny shoes glinting in the evening sun as if they were happy too. "And will the skull be OK for your show?"

"Of course, Mr Henry, it's going to be a *fantastic* start to the act." Potty was thrilled that it was all coming together. "But we will need to perform the trick at night-time."

"That is not a problem. You will appear at the end of the show. There is a juggler first, then the mayor is going to come on and say

112

something rather boring, then you."

"We will need to have the Queen sitting just to the left of the building, in a specially marked seat," instructed Potty. "That way she will be in the perfect spot to witness the museum's disappearance."

"I imagine you're expecting a little medal for this, eh, Mr Potty?" said Henry, nudging the performer. "Heh heh – a reward for all that hard work?"

Uncle Potty was taken aback. "No no! I had nothing like that in mind. I just want to put on a good show."

"Maybe a knighthood instead, hmm?"

Esmé interrupted. "We're here to do the best we can, Mr Henry, and if I may speak

for Potty, I believe he has no interest in titles or medals."

Henry raised his eyebrows. "I admire your integrity, each one of you. Now, the light is starting to fade, so let's begin rehearsals," he beamed. "I'll just get that crystal skull and put it into place out at the front. It'll be a show to remember, Mr Potty."

"*In all totality!*" announced Potty in the spotlight, swinging his magic wand in the air as if he was the conductor of a small orchestra. He was wearing a new purple cape over his tweed suit, trimmed with yellow pom-poms.

Monty Pepper stood next to him, gazing

114

up at the great magician in awe, awaiting instructions. He was dressed in a silver cape today, which made him look as if he had been wrapped in cooking foil.

"Welcome," Potty told the crowd – which this afternoon consisted of just Esmé and Henry J. Henry – "to the show of a lifetime… nay, an epoch."

Esmé sat watching the trick from a plastic chair, thrilled to be sitting in the exact spot the Queen would occupy in precisely two days' time.

Potty and Monty stood on the main path in front of the museum, behind the crystal skull, which was perched on a plump velvet cushion on a small plinth. It glinted in the spotlight. To Potty's right was the *Plants from Really Really Ancient Times* display. To his left stood two mammoth security guards, Trevor and Heather Bonce, making sure that the skull was protected at all times. They had matching bumbags with the words *Bonce Security*™ sewn on them in curly gold lettering.

"And now, witness the incredible... the magical... crystal skull," said Potty, pointing to the precious slab of crystal. Monty nodded his head and also pointed to the skull with his own magic wand, then shot a quick glance at Esmé, who gave him an encouraging smirk.

"The skull hails from the ancient *Mexica*

civilisation," said Potty, who liked to be informative as well as entertaining. "The *Mexica* people believed the crystal skull was imbued with a spirit that would grant them good fortune and *real* fortune."

Here, Potty produced a pound coin from behind Monty's ear. "But what happens at dusk," asked Potty, his long hands fluttering over the top of the skull, "when the sun goes down and the spirits themselves make merry?"

The trick was timed to coincide exactly with sunset; the light was already fading and Uncle Potty raised his hands slowly above his head. Monty, after a slight pause, did the same. Then both Potty and Monty

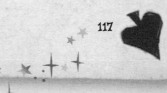

clapped their hands twice, in unison.

"Darkness!" Potty shouted as the spotlights went out. "We have embraced the night!"

The performers were plunged into the dark for a couple of seconds, then a bright white spotlight fell on the plinth – and the cushion was bare. Potty had managed to make the crystal skull disappear in record time.

Esmé stood up and started to applaud. "Hurray!" she shouted, eager to express her admiration. As she looked to her left, Esmé noticed that Henry J. Henry was standing beside her.

"A simply wonderful act," he said, grinning at Esmé.

The spotlight widened so that both Potty and Monty were illuminated.

"I will now find my magic wand and make the skull disappear!" said Potty. He smiled at the crowd while fishing in his cape.

Monty moved over and nudged his uncle in the ribs.

"Potty," he muttered, "the skull has *already* disappeared!"

"What?" answered the Potty Magician. "That can't be..." He glanced at the plinth in disbelief. Then he froze, mouth open.

Henry J. Henry, realising all was not as it should be, started walking towards him. "Has something gone wrong?" he asked.

Esmé followed Henry.

"What's happening?" she asked.

"I do apologise," Potty addressed Henry J. Henry, "but we seem to have lost the crystal skull."

"You are joking, of course," replied Henry, seeming a little confused.

"Are you sure it's lost?" asked Esmé. "Isn't it in your cape?

But the look on Monty and Potty's faces suggested that this was not a joke and that the skull was most *definitely* lost.

"I don't understand it," said Potty. "This has never happened to me before, Mr Henry. I am so terribly sorry."

But Henry was not happy, despite Potty's apologies.

"I put my trust in you, old sport," he said, his eyes narrowing. "I lent you that skull so that your trick would be the greatest. You knew it was not just a fabulous historical object, valuable to scientists and the public alike. You knew it was – *is* – worth a great deal of money. I put it to you that you have stolen the skull."

"This is simply not true!" exclaimed Potty.

"Mr Potty, I showed you the exhibits myself and in confidence. I told you how precious the skull was. You – yes, *you* – have decided to repay me by snatching this valuable piece."

Esmé gasped. How had he come to

this conclusion? Potty had never stolen anything in his life.

"You may gasp, little girl, but it is the truth," hissed Henry. "Potty has masterminded a devious plan, and I am horrified. Never trust a magician. Guards, seize him!"

Heather and Trevor Bonce moved in and grabbed Potty by the shoulders. Monty ran to his sister's side.

"Unhand me, you fools!" Potty shouted to the guards as they tussled with both him and his satin cape. "Henry, I can *prove* I didn't steal the skull."

"Nonsense. You're as guilty as can be."

"Let Potty show you he hasn't got it," pleaded Esmé.

"But Potty is a magician," said Henry, turning round to Esmé. "He fools people for a living. He hides a wand here, a silk scarf there – his whole life is spent tricking people."

Esmé tried to appeal to reason for the last time. "There has simply been a mistake, Mr Henry."

"It's a matter for the police now," spat the museum boss as the Bonces dragged Potty away.

"This is madness, Mr Henry!" yelled Monty.

Potty struggled, but the guards' grip was far too strong, probably due to the fact that they had biceps as big as cowbells. In an instant, they bundled Potty into a waiting van, which sped off quickly.

Esmé grabbed Monty before Henry spotted them and they both hid behind a Corinthian pillar.

"What are we going to do?" she asked. "We both know Potty didn't steal the skull."

Monty nodded.

"I've got a nasty feeling that Henry made the skull disappear using his magician's skills – and so *he* must still have it somewhere," said Esmé.

Monty agreed. "One moment it was there, the next moment it was gone."

"We need to find the skull, then present it to Henry as proof."

"But how?"

"We dash into the museum and start looking there, before anyone spots us," said Esmé, thinking fast. "It's bound to be nearby. This is the perfect opportunity."

Monty sighed. "We have to save Potty."

Esmé held his hand and the two Pepper twins scuttled off through the main doors and into the vastness of the Mega-Million Super Museum, desperate to uncover the truth.

An excerpt from

Dr Pompkins – Totality Magic

TRICK: Mind Magic Spook Tumbler

Find a glass tumbler and put it upside down on a
table in front of your crowd. Now find a small object
in your possession, such as a piece of jewellery. Take
the object in your hands, roll it about a bit and talk
about how many magical vibes it has. Now put the
object on the table and choose six people from your
audience to come up. Turn your back while someone
from the small group puts that object under the
tumbler, supervised by your assistant, and then
turn round again. Now tell them that using *mind
magic*, you will guess *who* put the object under the
tumbler when your back was turned. Tell each of
the six people to place an index finger slowly on the

inverted tumbler to create more magical vibes, and you will correctly guess who it was who placed the object there. Your audience will be astonished when you are right!

The secret is that your assistant will have seen who placed the object under the tumbler, and you have told said helper in advance to sniff just as the tumbler is touched by the person who placed the object.

———

Salutations! It's a winner!

Spookery

The midnight spook show was once a very popular form of entertainment. During the evening, a magician would entertain a drawing room full of people with the summoning of ghosts: noises would be heard from inside empty cupboards, strange breezes would be felt from nowhere at all, tables would suddenly tip up or objects fly around the room. These tricks were just that – *tricks* – but some folk believed the magician to have supernatural powers and gave him all their money.

Frolicsome as ghosties seem, never pretend you are a spook. It will not bring you riches – it will cause countless problems instead. If you do want to perform some of the *mind-magic* tricks we have in here, make sure that your audience know this is just entertainment and you are no more psychic and supernatural than anyone else.

In all totality,

Dr Pompkins

CHAPTER SEVEN

Warthogs

Henry J. Henry stood next to the Bonces outside the museum while Potty was carted away in the van. Henry had forgotten, for the moment, about Esmé and Monty.

Now the Pepper twins were inside the museum, they realised how cold and dark it was at night. Monty shivered. The walls, lit by moonlight from windows in the ceiling, looked a ghostly blue-white. The marble

seemed to glow in the dark and the smell of citrus cleaning fluid stung the air.

"Now, first things first," said Esmé, as they walked along one of the many corridors. "Did you see Henry tamper with the skull or the cushion before the rehearsal?"

"I didn't notice anything," replied Monty. "Potty and I were too busy gearing up for the trick."

"He *must* have used his magician's skills," said Esmé. "What could he have done?"

"Hole in the cushion?" ventured Monty.

"No, you would have noticed."

"Trapdoor in the ground?"

"*Outside* the museum?" asked Esmé. "The ground looks pretty solid."

"It might *look* like solid ground," replied Monty, "but in my experience, trapdoors can be anywhere."

"Well, it's a possibility," said Esmé. "But where could Henry have put the skull once it had disappeared?"

Monty thought hard. "In a mysterious cupboard?"

"Hang on!" Esmé had had a brainwave. "Didn't Sir Hans Toast devise a special code inside the museum?"

"Yes, and we saw it by Dr Dee's mirror, I'm sure of it, even though Henry said it was something to do with the audio tour."

"Somehow the code reveals where the secret passageways are – it said so in my

library book," said Esmé excitedly. "Now, Henry claimed that he didn't know about any passageways or tunnels. But if he *did...*"

"He would have hidden the skull there! Perfect, Es."

"All we have to do is find the mirror and read the code."

"Let's go!"

The Pepper twins set off in the direction of the *Big Ruffled Collars* room to find the obsidian mirror – the one that Henry had described as boring. A side entrance led them through previously unseen exhibits this time, and in the dim light Monty and Esmé started to feel nervous. They weren't

at all sure where they were going. To begin
with, they came across a small room that
was lined with tiny objects. When Monty
looked closely, he could see, pinned up on
the wall, several rows of miniature, brightly
coloured skeletons made from yarn or
paper, grinning wildly at him.

"Where are we?" Monty asked Esmé, his
voice quivering.

Esmé pulled out the small torch that
she still had in her cagoule pocket, causing
the packet of strawberry chews to fall on to
the floor.

"It says, 'We are celebrating Mexico's
Day of the Dead.'"

Monty gulped loudly.

"Have a chew," said Esmé, picking up the packet. "It might calm your nerves."

Monty took a sweet for now, and put the rest in his trouser pocket for later.

"Let's hurry," urged Esmé, walking swiftly through the room and straight into the next. It was dark here too, but bigger. Enormous carved heads had been placed on sticks and placed all round the room.

Esmé used her torch to read the sign on the wall.

"'African face masks,'" she said, "'traditionally used to symbolise spirits.'"

"Oh no." Monty was still flustered by the skeletons.

"'These are still common in certain parts

of Africa,'" read Esmé, trying to stay calm. "'They are used in rituals and ceremonies. Tribal chiefs wear them. They are very high status.'"

Monty still looked uncomfortable.

"That one looks like a warthog – what does it say?" he asked.

"'Its fangs are greatly feared.'"

"I agree... they look frightening to me," mumbled Monty.

"This is half crocodile, half Spirit of Strength," said Esmé, pointing to a particularly terrifying wooden mask that had pointy jaws and long twigs sprouting from its ears.

Crashhhherrrreugh!

The sound made both Esmé and Monty jump and they turned to see the two Bonce security guards running into the room and knocking over a huge mask.

"Bother," said Trevor.

"Drat," said Heather. "Where are the twins? We've got to find 'em; Henry told us to."

"I can't see anything in here," said Trevor. "Maybe I can sniff 'em out. What do kids smell like?"

"Sweets, mostly," replied Heather.

Esmé and Monty exchanged glances, grabbed a mask each and stood behind them, absolutely still.

Together, Bonce Security™ started

fumbling about the room, trying not to knock over more huge masks.

"What are these things? Roman shields?" asked Heather.

"I was never very good at history," said Trevor. "Are you sure they're not mummies?"

Heather stopped for a moment.

Esmé tried not to move a muscle.

"I'm sure I can smell something over here, Trev," said Heather, who was alarmingly close to the Pepper twins.

Trevor walked slowly towards Monty, then gave one almighty sniff. "Strawberry, most definitely," he said. "The smell of sweeties."

Esmé knew they were just about to be discovered. So, shielded by the giant mask, she lined the torch up behind the eye holes and turned it on full beam.

"*Roooooaaaarrr!*" she shouted.

Monty took one look at his sister, realised what was happening, and joined in, equally loudly.

"*Roooooaaaarrrrgghhhh!*" he thundered, and took a swipe at Trevor and Heather Bonce with his free hand.

"Aaargh!" screamed Heather.

"Let's scarper!" yelled Trevor, and the poor frightened Bonces dashed out of the room.

The Pepper twins lowered their masks.

"Not *incredibly* bright, are they?" laughed Esmé.

"But it's not going to take them long to catch up with us, sis," warned Monty.

"You're right. We need to get to the mirror fast. It must be near here somewhere," said Esmé, putting her mask on the floor. "Come on."

"Don't you think we should hang on to these?" asked Monty, still clutching his mask.

"No, they might weigh us down."

Monty stopped to think.

"We are doing the right thing, aren't we, Es? Do we definitely *know* that Henry has hidden the skull in the museum? Maybe he's put it in a suitcase, got his passport and made for the nearest airport."

"I did think of that." said Esmé. "But why would Henry want to go anywhere? He wants to put on an incredible, world-beating royal opening right *here*. He wouldn't leave town. No, the skull must be nearby. We must hurry."

Monty dropped his mask, and the Pepper twins ran. It did not take long before they found the *Big Ruffled Collars* room – and Dr Dee's mirror.

The black mirror glimmered, despite being surrounded by dull light. Esmé looked at the code on the information panel. She tried to read it forwards,

143

then backwards – but it looked like gobbledygook.

"What do the symbols say, Esmé?" asked Monty.

Esmé bit her lower lip – the code was a jumble. How had she been so silly as to think that she could decipher it in minutes? This was a task that took people – experts – months, *years* even.

"I'm not sure..." she said.

"Come on, Es, we haven't got all day," Monty said. "Where are the secret passageways?"

Esmé squinted at the panel, flummoxed. It was no use – the symbols were all over the place. None of them seemed to be repeated in the way a letter would be in a sentence. Maybe this wasn't a language after all, but a grand practical joke.

"I'm sorry, Monty, I don't know."

Monty was upset. "But we have to find out," he urged. "We *have* to get the skull and rescue Potty! The Bonces will catch up with us sooner or later and we'll be thrown in jail with Potty for breaking and entering, or stealing African face masks... or *anything*."

Esmé sighed. "It's, erm, I just can't..." she trailed off. "Wait a moment."

Monty noticed that she was squinting at the code again, her head tilting a little to the left.

"Have you got it?" he asked.

"Nearly," Esmé said, concentrating hard. Then her face broke into a broad smile. "That's it! It's not an actual *code* – the symbols don't mean anything in themselves."

"Really?" said Monty.

"It's *much* simpler than that. The symbols aren't letters that make up words to form a sentence. If you half-close your eyes, they turn into a map of the secret passageways that are right underneath us. And if I am correct, what we're standing on here..."

Esmé leant over to press a small button that was hidden at the base of the display cabinet.

"Is a trapdoor."

All of a sudden, a hatch beneath their feet opened and the Pepper twins dropped to the passageway below. A soft landing came by way of a large pile of feather pillows. A semi-startled Monty glanced at a label that was attached to one of them. It said:

**A GIFT TO THE NATION
FROM THE QUEEN AND KING OF PERU.
FOR MUSEUM USE ONLY.
NO PETS, PLEASE.**

Esmé glanced around. They had found the secret passageway.

An excerpt from

Dr Pompkins – Totality Magic

TRICK: Eggs from a Hat

Invite two persons from the audience on to the stage and show them a nice big hat. From it you produce an egg, then another, then another and so forth.

As you do, you hand the egg to person 1, who then has to pass it to person 2. You instruct both *never* to drop the eggs, which, nonetheless, just keep on coming.

And this goes on until person 1 is rapidly dropping eggs here, there and everywhere, to the amusement of the audience. Their enjoyment comes from the almost endless number of *oeufs* produced from your hat – and the surprise on the helpers' faces.

slit in hat lining

The secret of where all the eggs are coming from lies in the hat, which has a specially prepared inner lining with a slit in the crown, in which you have previously stashed them. Sewing and handicrafts will help you, and presentation is the key to this trick. Keep up the pace.

This trick was made famous by the Great Raymondue-Fondue, who performed it throughout the world and on the outskirts of Wolverhampton. He was exceptionally fast with the eggs.

Organisation

It is important to be organised when you are filing your tricks and storing them. One misplaced wand or a bunch of silk flowers in the wrong place and you will lose precious time a-searching, and not performing. I once tried to produce a rabbit from a hat at a dinner party in Leicester, only to find I had made a can of spaghetti hoops appear from a sandwich. Of course I turned it all around with instant patter, but I was a little embarrassed.

Find some shoe boxes or similar – if the boxes are roughly the same size they are easier to store – and keep your props in them. Label the outside of each box clearly, so you know what is in there. That way you will not be tripped up by Life's Certain Chaos.

In all totality,

Dr Pompkins

CHAPTER EIGHT

One Smells a Rat

Briiing briiing! Briiing briiing!

Her Majesty the Queen looked at the telephone. Seated in her small study at the palace, the phone was not far away, but she hesitated before picking it up.

The Queen did not like it when anyone called on the private number – she was always mistrustful. She hoped it wasn't the blasted prime minister again, telling her about all the great policies he'd put in place that day in order to keep the price of butter up and the cost of legwarmers down. Or was it one of those sportspeople, Lord So-and-So, who wanted to build a new stadium so people could practise crazy golf or Yahtzee. The Queen had had quite enough of sport since those blasted Olympics.

And so it was a great relief to Her Majesty when she heard the voice of Henry J. Henry on the other line. She hoped that he'd have an update about the royal opening – maybe some extra-comfy seats and free Twix bars to anyone whose father had once been king.

"There's been a small problem," Henry's voice quavered.

"What is it, Mr Henry J. Henry?" answered the Queen, irritated that he was bothering her with difficulties.

"Please, just call me Mr Henry," simpered Henry.

"Mr Henry J. Henry," repeated the Queen.

"Or, just *Henry*?"

"One is calling you Mr Henry J. Henry, Mr Henry J. Henry, because one is the Queen."

"Some people simply call me—"

"Mr Henry J. Henry J. Henry," said the Queen, starting to lose patience. "Please get to the point."

"The Potty Magician – who as you know was to perform here the day after tomorrow – has had a little, um, accident," said Henry. "He tripped over a spoon and broke his leg so he can't perform at the royal opening."

"Oh." The Queen was disappointed. She had been a keen fan of the Potty Magician since his brief appearance on the *Britain's Gone Magic!* TV show six months ago, when he turned a turnip into a Thai banquet for two. "Can't he use crutches?" she said, exasperated. "Or simply sit down?"

"Erm... the fracture is extremely serious," replied Henry. "Actually, there are two fractures, maybe three. And his arms don't look too good, either."

"You said he fell over a *spoon*?" The Queen did not quite believe her royal ears.

"Well, it was a big spoon, Your Majesty – more like a catering spoon. He's probably broken his nose as well."

"Would it be possible to have Potty beamed in by satellite from his hospital bed?"

Henry was silent. *Hospital* – he hadn't thought of that one.

"He is *in* hospital, isn't he?" enquired the Queen.

"It's very far away," spluttered Henry. "Norfolk."

"Well, that doesn't matter as far as satellites are concerned, does it?" Her

Majesty was becoming more and more irate. "He could be in blasted Timbuktu and all you'd need would be a camera and a live link-up. Mr Henry J. Henry J. Henry, one is *not* amused."

"I could find someone else..."

"One is disappointed," said the Queen. "But one shall still be visiting the day after tomorrow, as it is one's jewels you're showing, after all."

The Queen put the phone down. Something was not right, but she could not put her royal finger on it. Henry's story about Potty's injuries was rather far-fetched – was he being entirely truthful?

"One smells a rat..." she said to herself.

Many years ago, when the Queen had first ascended the throne, she had found it hard to adjust to queenly life. The dinners with visiting dignitaries (she still didn't really know what a dignitary was) were long and boring. The food was always bland and the portions were small. She had to wave to strangers when she was out and about, which was very dreary and made her right wrist seize up in cold weather. She was never allowed to wear interesting clothes, or outrageous make-up, or stick her tongue out at the prime minster. Instead, Her Majesty had had to learn how to be pleasant, polite and punctual. So every now and then, when it all got a bit too much –

on an afternoon off (how she had at first hated saying "*orf*") or with a morning to spare – she decided to pep things up a little. On these occasions Her Majesty the Queen would take to the streets in secret, disguised as a punk rocker called Bert.

Bert had a green mohican and liked swigging fizzy pop from a can. But although it was great fun – and spitting in public became her speciality – the Queen soon found this costume was harder and harder to get away with. Bert's many punk friends started asking lots of awkward questions, such as why she never went to the 2000 Club where all the new bands played and why she pronounced *off* as *orf*.

And so, a little while later, the Queen decided to create Celia Nutkins. Celia liked wearing floral housecoats, lived on her own in a small flat, had a hamster named Bryan and was a whizz at cross-stitch (Celia, not the hamster).

After the phone call with Henry, the Queen knew that it was time for Celia Nutkins to make a short visit to the Mega-Million Super Museum, to find out just what on earth was going on.

Her Majesty opened the drawer in her study and took out a curly wig, housecoat, nylon skirt and trainers. It took mere seconds to become Celia.

"One is impressed," she murmured,

looking at herself in the mirror. Then she walked downstairs through the back exit so no one would see her go. Celia Nutkins pulled her old battered motorbike from the staff garage, swung herself on to the seat and zoomed off towards the Mega-Million Super Museum in search of the rat himself, Mr Henry J. Henry J. Henry.

An excerpt from

Dr Pompkins – Totality Magic

TRICK: Penny and Coat Hanger Trick

This trick uses simple physics, and it is a good way to start a show. Bend a metal coat hanger to make it more of a diamond shape. Place a penny on the hook of the coat hanger {fig. 1} and then spin the hanger, with the penny still balanced, round your index finger.

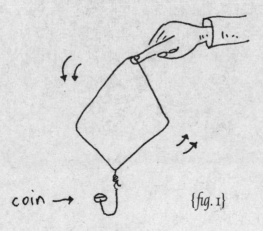

coin →   {fig. 1}

Practise this many times and the penny will stay on, defying gravity. This is good to perform in front of small children and excellent if you have just had a large fish supper and would rather not be too energetic with your act. I do hear that some magicians try and add coins to the pile, but I have found it rather tricky.

Confusion

I have seen some of the best conjurors perform around the world, as I have no doubt already informed you in earlier volumes, and some of their tricks I can decode, others I am simply befuddled by. The invention of the mobile phone means a thousand new magicians use phones for their tricks and have them ringing all over the stage – from trouser pockets, cardboard boxes, members of the audience or from inside small vegetables. Some magicians use technology to great advantage to update more traditional tricks. I myself find mobile phones confusing, with all those buttons and bleeps, so have decided not to use them. But if you can make a telephone

ring from a Staffordshire bull terrier, you will *wow* your
audience time and time again.

In all totality,

Dr Pompkins

CHAPTER NINE

The Hideaway

The Pepper twins found themselves in a long tunnel surrounded by a lot of dust – small dusty items, medium-sized dusty items and large dusty items. *Everything* was covered in a thick layer of dust. Even the walls had cobwebs on them. Dusty cobwebs.

The passageway stretched straight ahead, poorly lit by bare electric bulbs. It was the

perfect place to hide a crystal skull. Now all they had to do was find it.

Esmé and Monty started simply by walking.

"I hope the security guards don't know about this part of the building," said Monty as they travelled along the corridor.

"Me too," said Esmé, gripping Monty's arm. "We need to find the crystal skull as soon as possible."

The passageway was crammed with objects that were presumably too big, too dull, too strange or indeed far too dusty to be displayed in the museum itself. The first thing they came across, which almost

completely obstructed their way, was a giant ball shape wrapped in brown paper.

"It must be at least two metres wide," said Monty, intrigued by its size. "What is it?"

It was addressed to SIR HANS TOAST, HOLBORN, LONDON, ENGLAND and the sender was marked as SIR HANS TOAST, EXPLORER'S HUT, INNER COSTA RICA, CENTRAL AMERICA.

"Too big for a game of football," said Monty.

Esmé turned over the label that was attached to the wrapping. "It's a giant stone ball from the Costa Rican jungle," she remarked. "It says, 'Catalogue Number: HT 132,674 CR. Discovered in the 1930s when we were clearing the way for a banana plantation. Have not yet found out what it is used for. Am sending it back to London via boat in order to carry out more research. Signed Sir H. Toast.' Maybe he never found out anything more."

The Peppers squeezed past the ball shape and continued up the corridor.

The next object that lay directly in front of them was a stuffed rodent-like creature. Monty read the accompanying tag this time.

"'Catalogue Number: HT 104 JTM. Jeff the talking Mongoose was a phenomenon in Scotland in the early part of the 1900s. An animal that lived inside the wall of the family home, he told the family he was a ghost and used to play tricks on them,

similar to a poltergeist, but in mongoose form. Signed Sir H. Toast.'"

Monty turned and looked back the way they had come. "I'm certain I can hear footsteps," he whispered.

"Let's keep moving," said Esmé.

The Pepper twins hurried on through the dusty corridor, past a big stone object labelled CAVEMAN MOBILE and another bulky item called EARLY INCA TELEVISION SET. There were pots in a corner that were cracked and broken, and even several stuffed camels.

But no crystal skull.

Eventually, Esmé and Monty came to the end of the passageway, and a closed door.

A small metal nameplate read SIR HANS TOAST, MUSEUM FOUNDER.

"This looks like the entrance to Hans Toast's study," said Esmé excitedly. "I read about it in the library book. It was a very special place, but few knew its whereabouts. Toast used to sit down here for hours, cataloguing his treasures. I think Henry J. Henry *must* have known about this room all along. If he's the museum boss, there's no way it would still be a secret to him."

"Are you sure?" asked Monty.

"I have a strong feeling Henry knows everything about the museum," replied Esmé, trying the door.

"It's locked."

Monty turned round. "I can definitely hear those footsteps, Es," he whispered. "Come on, we haven't got much time. Try the door again."

Then Esmé remembered the penknife in the pocket of her cagoule, took it out and started to fiddle with the lock.

"Did the great escapologist, Maureen Houdini, teach you how to do that?" asked Monty. Esmé nodded as the door creaked open to reveal Sir Hans Toast's study.

As the Pepper twins entered, they saw it was lined with old wooden cabinets, comprising hundreds of drawers, each labelled on the outside. Also squeezed into the room was a bookcase and three glass cabinets containing stuffed birds – an emu, a cockatiel and a dodo. Framed paintings of exotic, richly coloured flowers were placed on the large oak desk in the centre of the room.

"Wow," said Monty. "I wish our magic shed looked like this."

"I wonder what's in those drawers. The crystal skull, maybe?" said Esmé, walking up to a wooden cabinet and looking at the labels. "Oh, I think it's all plant samples."

As she gazed at the Latin names in tiny handwriting, Esmé thought how exceptionally intelligent and interesting Sir Hans Toast must have been. She started to open some of the bigger drawers, just in case the skull had been hidden inside one of them.

Monty scanned the bookcase. "Ah!" he gasped, delighted. "There's an ancient copy of *Dr Pompkins – Totality Magic* in here."

"Just try finding the skull," replied his sister. "We haven't much time."

"Got to have a quick look," said Monty, unable to resist taking the copy from the shelf. "This is a newer edition of Pompkins than the one at home."

He grabbed the enormous book and took it eagerly to the desk.

"*How* is that going to help?" asked Esmé, exasperated, closing a drawer filled with fossilised stones.

"It's not as dusty as the others," said Monty. "And there's a bookmark. Someone must have read it recently."

Esmé joined Monty at the desk, as he carefully opened the book at the marked page. He slowly began to read aloud.

"'Trick: The Vanishing Skull.'"

Esmé and Monty looked at each other in disbelief.

"Maybe it's a coincidence," said Monty. "Perhaps it was Hans Toast's favourite trick."

But Esmé pointed to the bookmark, on which was printed BOOKMAGIC.COM.

"This book must have been used in the last few years," she said. "Hans Toast died in nineteen sixty-one. There was no internet then."

Monty flicked to the title page.

"Esme, there's another clue. A *gigantic* clue."

"What?"

"It says *This book belongs to Harry Starfeathers* in neat handwriting."

Monty showed the page to Esmé, who sank down in the ornate office chair. "This is our evidence that Henry stole the skull. He memorised the trick and used it!"

"We've still got to find the skull itself," sighed Monty.

"I've looked in most of these drawers," said Esmé. "It's not there."

"It's not in the stuffed emu, is it?" asked Monty, staring at the static bird in the glass cabinet.

"I don't know ab—"

The rattle of a doorknob stopped Esmé in mid-sentence and she looked round to see Henry J. Henry appear in the doorway. He was carrying something in a plastic bag and seemed as startled by their presence as they were by his.

"What are you two doing here?" Henry's expression turned from surprise to confusion, then anger. "Are you rummaging around in my personal affairs?"

Esmé shook her head; Monty could only let out a squeak.

"As if your thieving Uncle Potty wasn't bad enough," hissed Henry. "Get out of my office!"

"I thought it was Sir Hans Toast's office," replied Esmé bravely.

"Er, yes – well, of course it *was*."

Then Henry saw the magic book lying open on the oak desk. He was going to ask what the Pepper twins were doing with it, but he already knew.

"*What?* Now, play fair, young sports. You must not search out the magician's secrets – *indocilis privata loqui*."

"Never trust a locust," Monty whispered to Esmé, by way of explanation. "I've just translated it from the Greek for you."

"I think you mean *not apt to disclose secrets*," corrected Esmé. "From the Latin – the magician's code."

"Oh yes," said Monty, quietly.

Esmé could see by the look on Henry's face that he realised he had been found out.

"We know it was you that stole the crystal skull and not Potty," she said, pointing a finger at the museum boss. "Mr Henry, I accuse you of bookmarking the trick and performing it yourself while Potty was rehearsing. Now all we need to find is the skull and we will phone the police."

Henry J. Henry gulped. There was a rustling sound as he tried to hide the plastic bag behind his back.

"What's that noise?" asked Monty.

"Mice," said Henry.

"You are trying to conceal something in that plastic bag, Mr Henry," said Esmé, who had a strong hunch it was the crystal skull.

"Erm..." Henry had arrived at the office red-handed. He had been intending to place the skull in the bottom desk drawer, where he could lock it out of the way for the time being, then sell it to the particularly keen collector he had been having high-level talks with.

"Honestly, young sports, we have a problem down here with vermin. There are hundreds of them. They come and go through the statue of the Ancient Egyptian God Min."

"What are you hiding behind your back?" repeated Esmé.

"Nothing," said Henry, as he edged slowly towards the bookcase. A moment later, he had pressed a concealed button and a ladder swiftly descended from the ceiling.

"Goodbye, children!" he shouted as he started to climb upwards.

"Not so fast," said Monty, who had now realised what was in the bag. "You've got the crystal sku—"

But Henry had already disappeared through a hole in the ceiling.

"What do we do now?" Monty asked his sister.

"Follow him!" yelled Esmé, and the twins pursued Henry up the ladder and back to the ground floor of the museum.

Dr Pompkins – Totality Magic

TRICK: Church Steeple

This trick appears to be like hypnotism – if your patter is good enough to convince the audience.

Ask a friend casually if you could try a little _instant hypnosis_ while giving assurances that it's safe and nothing harmful will happen. Ask this friend to fold his or her hands together, weaving the fingers and clasping them tightly. After a few moments of doing this, tell him or her to raise both index fingers so they stick up and are ideally about two centimetres apart – the _church and steeple_ shape {fig. 1}.

{fig. 1}

Now move your hands slowly over your friend's (without touching them) and say, "Your index fingers will touch, my dear friend and chum. Try to fight it, but they will touch."

Slowly, but inevitably, your friend's index fingers will begin to move towards each other. Keep telling your friend to concentrate on his or her fingers and soon the fingers _will_ touch {fig. 2}.

{fig. 2}

This is just pure biology – but it should still be practised a few times beforehand.

Animals

Magicians used to have pockets full of white rabbits, and waistcoats stuffed with doves. Decades ago – up to the 1970s, I imagine – animals were used in tricks willy-nilly and nobody minded at all. Large animals, such as lions, elephants and snakes, were also used by the more exotic performers of yesteryear. However, now it is the Modern Age and the vast population does not like the thought of cruelty to animals. Does the stage pet have enough rest and a large enough supply of squeaky toys to keep it happy? Will it expire from the pressures of fame if it performs a tour of the Crawley area? I am happy to give up my box of mice and declare myself an animal-free zone. I hope you will too. While pets are nice, they often bite you or wee near your packed lunch.

In all totality,

Dr Pompkins

CHAPTER TEN

Mrs Celia Nutkins

The ladder led up to a covered opening on the ground floor, near the museum's central marble staircase. This is where the Pepper twins now stood, wondering what to do next. They were, of course, in hot pursuit of Henry J. Henry, but he was nowhere to be seen.

"He might have gone up to the next

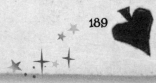

floor," suggested Monty, looking in the direction of the staircase.

"He could have gone *anywhere*," replied Esmé. "But we'll give upstairs a shot."

As the twins ran over to the steps, they crashed straight into a woman in a floral housecoat.

"Sorry, madam," said Esmé. "We're in a rush."

"Ah, a moment, please" replied Mrs Celia Nutkins, who was not used to people barging into her. "You may be able to help one."

"I'm afraid we have t—"

"One's name is Mrs Celia Nutkins and one is looking for a Henry J. Henry," said the woman in a slow, measured tone.

"So are we, Mrs Nutkins," said Monty. "But he's disappeared and we haven't much time."

"If you please, one needs a little information," said Mrs Nutkins, who refused to be hurried. "Do you know what happened to a man named the *Potty Magician*?"

Monty was suspicious. "You haven't been sent here by someone from the council called Jeremy, have you?"

"Of course not," came the reply. "But someone has told one that Potty has been injured and he can't perform."

Esmé was shocked to hear this. "No – he wasn't hurt," she said. "He's been taken to the local police station."

"The police station?" repeated Mrs Nutkins. "One heard that he is in hospital in Norfolk with a broken leg. And his arms are looking a bit dodgy too, apparently. There was nothing to suggest that he had engaged in any criminal activity."

Esmé wrinkled her forehead. "Who did you hear this from?"

"Why, Henry J. Henry, of course," replied Mrs Nutkins. "On the telephone. That's why one wants to find him and sort it out."

Esmé wondered why Henry had phoned this person, this Celia Nutkins, to say that Uncle Potty was out of action. What was her part in all of this?

"As far as we know, Uncle Potty was accused of a crime that he did not commit and was sent away," Esmé explained. "But we know who did it and we are right in the middle of catching him. I think you have been lied to, Mrs Nutkins."

Mrs Nutkins's eyebrows rose; she was becoming more and more annoyed. Her instinct had been right – Henry J. Henry had been telling porky pies, and she did not like it.

"*Lied to...*" she huffed, putting two and two together. "So, can one hazard a guess that it's the same Mr Henry you're chasing? Is he... *in deep?*"

Esmé nodded.

"The plot thickens," Mrs Nutkins continued. "Mr Henry J. Henry J. Henry seems to have framed the Potty Magician, lied to one about it and is now on the run – is one right?"

"In all totality," said Monty, impressed with Mrs Nutkins' powers of deduction.

In minutes, Esmé, Monty and Mrs Nutkins had worked out what was going on. Esmé explained in detail what had happened to Potty during rehearsals, how she and Monty had found the secret passageway and Sir Hans Toast's office, and how Henry had walked in with the skull in a plastic bag.

"Well, we must join forces," said Mrs

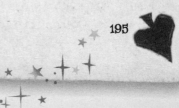

Nutkins. "We are both very cross with Mr Henry J. Whatnot, so he must be brought to justice."

But Esmé felt there was just one more thing left to discover.

"So you know who we are," she said, "but who exactly are *you*? *Why* exactly was Mr Henry calling you to say Potty was in hospital?"

"Erm..." answered the Queen. "Can you keep a secret?"

Monty and Esmé both nodded.

"Are you familiar with the Wealth and Wisdom Zone? The Crown Jewels, the sparkly bits, the general *bling* of it all?"

The Peppers continued to nod.

The Queen bent down and whispered. "Well, all that stuff belongs to one. One is the Queen. Her Maj."

Monty's eyes almost popped out of his head. Esmé had been wondering why Mrs Nutkins possessed such a refined air and a habit of not being able to say the word *I*. Now she knew. Monty gave a little bow; and Esmé bobbed a curtsy.

"Oh, tish now, enough of that," said the Queen modestly. "Let's go and find Mr Henry J. Henry J. Henry, and pronto."

Esmé, Monty and Her Majesty the Queen ran up the marble steps and began their search for Henry. At the top of the stairs

were two corridors, one leading to the right, another to the left.

"Which one should one take?" asked Her Maj.

"I'm not sure," replied Monty.

Esmé started sniffing.

"What are you doing?" asked her brother.

Within moments it became clear. There was a smell – a lingering, expensive, powdery essence of flowers and musk, teamed with the finest patchouli from the dusky mountains of Birmingham. Of course – it was Henry's aftershave, *Toujours, Matey*. And it was *definitely* hanging around in the right-hand corridor, so they all made a dash for it.

"What will Henry do when he sees us?" Monty was beginning to panic again. "He's going to be very angry."

"Not to worry," said the Queen. "One will tell him what's what and he will soon see sense."

Esmé wondered why Her Majesty was so sure about that.

No sooner had the trio walked a few paces in the murky light of this particular part of the museum, they spotted trouble ahead – Bonce Security™.

"Oh no," wailed Monty.

"Found ya!" said Trevor Bonce, running towards them.

"Can we go back?" asked Esmé, but it

was too late. Heather Bonce had grabbed her wrist.

"Get *orf*!" cried the Queen, as Trevor tried to get her into a headlock. "Do you know who one is?"

Dr Pompkins – Totality Magic

TRICK: Magic Sachet

You will need a clear plastic drinks bottle for this trick, plus a condiment sachet, which can usually be found in fast-food outlets. Ketchup or salad cream, it does not matter what is in it.

First, take the label off the bottle, then fill it almost entirely with cold tap water. Insert the sachet – note: it should float at the top of the bottle.

Now find a friend and tell him or her that you have magical fingers (if that is not common knowledge already) and that you will make the sachet in the bottle fall and rise at your command. Holding the base of the bottle with your left hand, as if to steady it, apply gentle squeezing pressure – with practice, onlookers should not be able to detect this subtle movement.

With your right hand in mid-air, guide the sachet upwards – if you decrease the pressure inside the bottle, the sachet should float slowly downwards. To make the sachet stop in the middle of the bottle, you need to apply just the right amount of pressure.

How your chum will marvel at your powers.

Leaflet-eering

Self-promotion is often key when there is magic at hand. In one of my books, _A Dr Pompkins Treasury_, I told you how to create a magic poster for your performances. Now I will tell you about leaflets. You can make your own flyers and hand them out at school. Maybe you can also set up a show during the lunch break – if the your teachers will allow it – or after school near the canteen. State who you are, what sort of magic you perform and maybe find yourself a logo – something swirly, a curlicue or illuminated letter. Be bold! No one wants to see a shy magician, someone who won't say boo to a goose. Be proud! Tell people your magic is really good. Practise! And if you have leftover flyers at any point, they are always handy when you need to redecorate a bathroom.

In all totality,

Dr Pompkins

CHAPTER ELEVEN

Bonce Security™ in Action

While Trevor struggled with the Queen, Heather Bonce held Esmé with one arm and Monty with the other, then lifted both off the ground by their waists.

"I've got the little ones, Trev."

Esmé and Monty tried to struggle free, but to no avail.

Within moments, however, the Queen

204

had managed to wriggle out of Trevor's headlock with a few deft moves.

"Excuse one," she said, snapping at the Bonces. "But what gives you the right to think you can grapple with people like that in this day and age? We have rights, you know."

"We 'ave been ordered to take you to see Mr 'Enry," said Trevor. "'E's in the Pottery Room over there."

Trevor pointed to a half-open door along the corridor, from which a dull grey light spilled.

"Funnily enough," said the Queen, "that is just the person one wishes to see."

The Queen marched off up the hallway

then turned to see the children still in the clutches of Heather Bonce.

"Does one have to explain oneself more clearly?" she asked. "Hands *orf* the children. *Put them down.* One has friends in very high places, so please do as one says, then one won't cause you any more aggro. *Comprendez?*"

Trevor and Heather Bonce – normally two brawny lumps of high-quality brawniness with very little brain to speak of – were cowed for once. And for some reason, they knew that this woman in the floral housecoat meant business, whoever she was. Heather dropped Esmé and Monty immediately, and the twins ran towards the Queen.

"Thank you," Her Majesty replied graciously, and together she and the Peppers walked up to the open door and went inside.

The Pottery Room was a dingy place where, it seemed to Esmé, quite uninspiring pieces of terracotta were displayed.

As they entered, Henry was standing in the middle of the room, the carrier bag in his hand, waiting.

"I've been expecting you," he said. "But it's taken you an awfully long time to get here."

Esmé wondered *why* he had been waiting and had not just run out of the museum

towards freedom. "We bumped into… an old friend," she told Henry.

The Queen winked under her curly wig, but Henry was not fooled by her disguise.

"Good evening, Your Majesty," he said, bowing. "I suppose these children have told you everything. They may even have convinced you that they are somehow in the right – and I am somehow in the wrong."

The Queen simply smiled.

"I can assure you, madam…" Henry trailed off. "Oh, what's the point? I *am* in the wrong and there is nothing that any of you can do about it. However, I *can* do something about it. I'm going to escape – yes, *escape*. I will leave this bloomin' museum, with all its bells and whistles, and go and live somewhere warm like Los Angeles."

Esmé and Monty looked at each other. They hadn't expected a speech.

Quick as a flash, Henry ran over to the open window in the far wall and began scrambling through it towards the outside ledge.

"I'm going now. It's been nice working with you, old sport," he said, still simpering at the Queen. "It's not been so nice working with you two, though," Henry added rather pointedly to the Pepper twins. "Too clever for your own good."

Henry got out on to the window ledge – still holding the carrier bag – and stood up.

"What should we do about the skull?" Monty whispered to his sister.

"Let him take it," said Esmé. "He's on a high window ledge. Trying to get the skull now would be dangerous."

"But we *have* to save Potty –" Monty was adamant – "and the skull is our proof."

"Now, whatever you're think—" But before Esmé could say any more, Monty was climbing out on to the window ledge in a bid to grab the skull.

"Stop!" cried Esmé.

"Get *orf* that ledge!" commanded the Queen, but it was too late, Monty had managed to stand up alongside the museum boss and was trying to talk him into handing over the skull.

"Mr Henry, we *need* the skull. Give me the bag."

"No, you silly child. Get away, I'm making my grand exit," Henry growled.

It seemed that Henry planned to jump from the window.

Monty looked down to the ground way, way below.

"But there's nothing to soften your fall," he said, suddenly unnerved to be up on this high ledge.

"Not yet, but I'm waiting for the Bonces to bring a mattress..." Henry clearly expected his crack security team to appear below at any second. "Get back

inside and, um, stand in the middle of the room."

At that moment Trevor and Heather Bonce walked through the door.

Henry saw them and shouted, "Bonce Security™! You're meant to be on the ground."

"Are we?" asked Heather.

"For sure?" asked Trevor.

As Henry argued with the Bonces, Monty took the opportunity to ease the plastic bag from the villain's fingers. Henry tried to hold on to the bag, but in the confusion he lost his grip.

"I've got it!" Monty called to Esmé. "Henry really is a butterfingers."

He clambered down from the window ledge and ran over to his sister and the Queen.

Henry was left standing on the ledge – perplexed and without the skull.

"This is not going to plan," he murmured to himself, just loud enough for everyone to hear. "The children were meant to be standing in the middle of the room, not joining me by the window."

He climbed down from the ledge sulkily and walked towards Monty.

"OK, give me the skull."

"No," said Monty.

"Trevor, Heather – *persuade* Monty to give me back the skull."

Trevor shot a look at the Queen and the Peppers, "I'm sorry, boss, but I'm not touching any of 'em," he said. "That lady says she 'as friends in 'igh places."

"*Who* pays your wages?"

Henry stood right in the centre of the room, glaring at his security team, as the Pepper twins and the Queen looked on.

Esmé suddenly remembered something Henry had said when they'd entered the Pottery Room – *I've been expecting you.* Henry had waited for Esmé and Monty in that room for a reason. And now Esmé looked more closely, she could see from the tiny marks on the floor that he and the Bonces had momentarily forgotten they were standing on one of Hans Toast's trapdoors. That must be the exact spot where Henry had wanted the Pepper twins to stand. Yet Monty now had the skull – an event that Henry had not foreseen – and Henry did not want to let the skull go. Everything made sense.

Esmé quickly looked around. Was there… could there be – *a secret button?* She scanned the room, looking at the display cabinets filled with earthenware – cracked plates and scuffed bowls. There had been a button by the obsidian mirror and one in Toast's study. *Surely…*

Ah! There it was – a small red disc on a display of plates.

Esmé nudged her brother.

"Monty – the display cabinet next to you," she whispered. "Press the red button, right now!"

Monty knew when to obey orders and did so straight away. Slowly, as Henry bickered with the Bonces about the skull, Monty edged closer to the cabinet. But Henry had decided enough was enough.

"Some security team *you* are," he said sarcastically to Trevor and Heather. "I'll just have to get it myself."

Quick as a flash, Monty made a move towards the button. He reached out and hit it with his index finger – but nothing happened.

Monty looked at Esmé anxiously.

"*Try again!*" she whispered.

Henry turned to Monty, and was just about to make a grab for the bag when Monty hit the button again, harder – with more success this time.

Caaaaaabhhhhhhooom!

The trapdoor opened with alarming speed. Henry and the Bonces dropped through the floor as fast as buttered toast.

"Dash it!" cried Henry as he fell.

After a moment's silence, the Queen and the Peppers heard a voice.

"Are you still going to escape, boss?" asked Trevor Bonce.

"I haven't got the skull, you *imbecile*. The

quick exit from the window ledge was all a bluff. The *children* were meant for the trapdoor, not us."

"Oh," said a baffled Trevor.

The Queen, Esmé and Monty walked up to the hole and peered down.

"Mr Henry J. Henry J. Henry," hollered the Queen, "you stole the crystal skull and you will be put in prison. The Potty Magician will return and perform a triumphant museum opening, of which you will no longer be a part. One hopes one will never hear from you again."

"I'm sorry, Your Majesty…"

"Sorry is not good enough, Mr Butterfingers," chuckled the Queen, who

had clearly heard of his nickname. Then she turned to Esmé and Monty. "One is *so* looking forward to Potty's show. Now why don't you go home and put the kettle on for him. Expect him back there in an hour – one will get one's people on to it."

"What do we do with this?" asked Monty, holding up the carrier bag that still contained the priceless skull.

"You leave that with one," said the Queen, winking for the second time and taking the bag. "One will put it somewhere safe."

Monty bowed deeply. "Thank you, ma'am. We are truly honoured."

"Now now, enough of the formalities,"

the Queen replied. "You have a show to prepare for."

An excerpt from

Dr Pompkins – Totality Magic

TRICK: Haunted Pendulum

Take a long piece of string from your pocket and ask someone in the audience for a ring.

Tie the ring to one end of the string, holding the other end so that it is like a pendulum. Tell everyone assembled that the ring is haunted and that the spirit it holds will answer questions. Get a volunteer to hold his or her hand, palm-side up, under the ring while asking a yes/no question, such as "Do I need to visit the dentist soon?"

The pendulum will swing back and forth for yes,

and it will swing in a circle for no. The wonder is, just thinking *yes* or *no* sets up the vibrations in your fingers that change the direction of the pendulum – so there's nothing to it. It simply means that **you** are in fact deciding whether or not friends or complete strangers should visit the dentist.

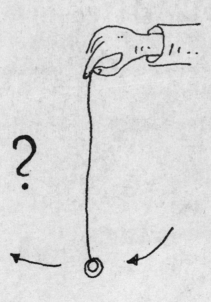

Our Finale

With alarming regularity we seem to be coming to the end
of another Dr Pompkins guide. I do hope that you, dearest
reader, a modern young person, have picked up some practical
advice that will put wind in your sails and make you become
the magician you've always wanted to be. I feel we have come
to a large bench by the side of our imaginary road, and we
should now park ourselves here and reflect.
"..."

Well, that was wonderful. Anon and adieu – please stay
in touch.

In all totality,

Dr Pompkins

CHAPTER TWELVE

A Few Hundred Doves and a Prince

"Are you *sure* this Celia Nutkins person wasn't from the council?"

It was past midnight and Potty was sitting, slightly bewildered, in the Peppers' kitchen. He had a lot to catch up on.

"In all honesty, it was the *real* Queen," explained Esmé. "She helped us find Henry J. Henry and get the crystal skull back."

Potty shifted in his seat and had a sip of tea.

"What a curious fellow that Mr Henry is," he slurped.

"And not a particularly nice one," said Esmé. "But when we go back tomorrow, at least he won't be anywhere near."

"It's late," said Potty. "We must get some shut-eye and then we will be refreshed for the show."

"I'd almost forgotten it was so soon," yawned Monty.

"As nice as it might have been to have a priceless object in my act, I'd better swap it for something *less* precious."

Esmé smiled, but she dared not think

about how much the skull was worth – just how much bother it had caused.

The Peppers and Potty arrived at the museum for the final run-through at midday the next day. By that time, there was already a large white van in the grounds.

"It's from Her Majesty," the driver called out of the cab. "A few hundred doves from Frogmore House for the finale. And a *very* special item, which is being hand-delivered."

Esmé heard the sound of a motorbike roaring up the driveway, turned and saw the Queen approaching.

"Hello, Esmé," said Her Majesty, as she took her bike helmet off.

"Hello, Your Majesty."

There was a pizza-delivery-style box on the back of the motorbike. "One has got something for the Potty Magician."

Potty stepped forward. "It's an honour to mee—"

"One does like your purple cape," interrupted the Queen, who was still dressed as Celia Nutkins. "One has one just like that at home. Now, on to important matters." She unclipped the box.

Potty took it and held it stiffly.

"Open it, won't you?"

So Potty carefully opened the box. Inside, something twinkled in the light.

"It's a crown..." Potty was stumped.

"Sorry, Your Majesty, I don't understand."

"*Philip!*" called the Queen in the direction of the van, and from the passenger seat appeared the Queen's husband.

"One has been trying to make him disappear for years, ahahaha!" laughed the Queen. "One thought he would be ideal for the first trick. He can wear the crown or not – whatever you choose. First, you make him vanish, then the museum – that *is* the act, is it not?"

"Yes, yes!" cried Potty. "Wonderful."

"Good afternoon, Mr Potty Magician," said Prince Philip, shaking hands with Potty. "I'm a big fan of yours and it will be a pleasure working with you – so my wife tells me."

Esmé and Monty smiled. Potty's act was going to be sensational.

And after the performance – in which Potty *did* make Prince Philip disappear first, then the whole museum – the audience were raving. The act had truly been a never-to-be-forgotten spectacle, and the doves at the end were the icing on the cake.

Potty was, as usual, modest and quick to praise Esmé and Monty – and the Queen – who had helped him put the show together. A man from the television introduced himself and gave Potty his business card. A famous pop star told Esmé she wanted

Potty to direct her next video. Monty ate a lot of after-show cakes and felt a bit sick as the evening wore on.

Walking back home through the darkening streets, Esmé, Monty and Potty were feeling on top of the world.

"I think that went well, did it not?" said Potty.

"In all totality," said Esmé.

"Shame Henry J. Henry missed it," Monty muttered.

"It's not a shame at all," said Esmé. "I'm glad he's in prison. He's where he deserves to be."

"I just meant it was a good show," said Monty.

Potty nodded his head. "While he's behind bars, maybe Mr Henry will think about his actions, realise he was wrong and come out a nicer and more generous human being."

Esmé thought Mr Henry might be too arrogant ever to feel genuinely sorry for what he'd done.

Beeeeee-eeeeeep! went a noise behind them, sharply and suddenly. All three turned to look at a car that had braked abruptly. It seemed that the driver had narrowly avoided running someone over.

"Do be careful, old sport," said a man's voice.

"Ruddy pedestrians!" the driver shouted back, shaking his fist as the man reached the

pavement and walked on in the direction of the museum.

Esmé couldn't be entirely *certain* in the darkness, but it looked as though the man was wearing an expensive grey suit. In fact, the man looked a little like Henry J. Henry, escaped from the clutches of the police and back to cause havoc at the Mega-Million Super Museum.

Of course it isn't, thought Esmé to herself. *It's late and you're tired.*

And she, Monty and Potty continued walking the short distance home.

THE
PEPPERS
AND THE
INTERNATIONAL MAGIC GUYS

Take a peek behind the scenes at the
wonderful world of THE PEPPERS…

The Pepper twins, Esmé and Monty, are
spending the holidays with their eccentric
Uncle Potty, a professional magician.

When they find out that Potty's beloved
magic club might have to close, the twins
are determined to use every trick in the
book to save it. But no one can find the
book, the escapologist is all tied up and
the human cannonball has had a nasty
accident. Can the twins still pull off the
performance of a lifetime?

A show-stopping story starring an
unbeatable double act.

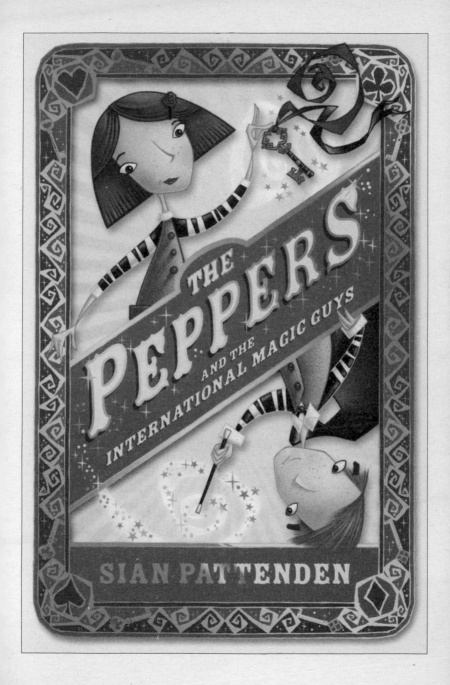

THE MAGICAL PEPPERS

AND THE ISLAND OF INVENTION

Join the Pepper twins on their next fantastic adventure full of magic and mayhem!

Esmé, Monty and their Uncle Potty have been summoned to the Sea Spray Theatre on the end of Crab Pie Pier. They're on a mission to keep the old theatre from closing and must perform the show of a lifetime to reel in the crowds.

But not everyone wants the theatre to survive and a certain someone is determined to sabotage the show, whatever the cost…

Add a strange island hideaway full of zany inventions, a hair-raising helicopter rescue-mission and the world's biggest goldfish bowl and the Peppers are in for an unforgettable summer!

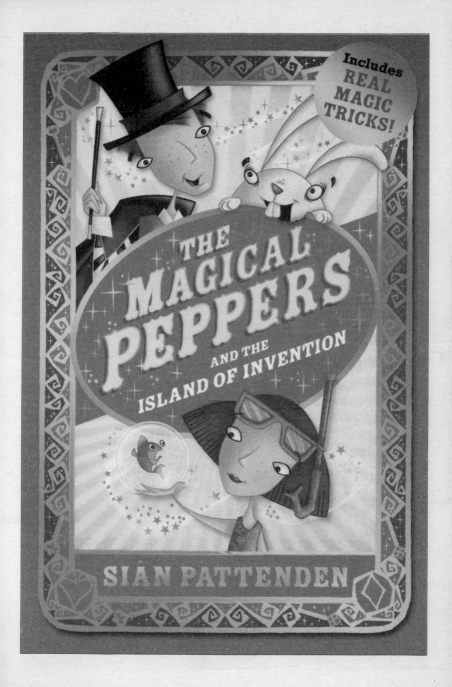

Includes
REAL
MAGIC
TRICKS!

THE
MAGICAL
PEPPERS
AND THE
ISLAND OF INVENTION

SIAN PATTENDEN

CASPER CANDLEWACKS in Death by PIGEON!

'A funny and engaging debut'
JEREMY STRONG

Ivan Brett